BEHIND THE SCENES AT

SCRAPHEAP

CHALLENGE

BEHIND THE SCENES AT

SCRAPHEAP CHALLENGE

ROBERT LLEWELLYN

First published in September 2001 by Channel 4 Books,
an imprint of Pan Macmillan Ltd, 20 New Wharf Road, London N1 9RR,
Basingstoke and Oxford.

Associated companies throughout the world.

www.panmacmillan.com

ISBN 0 7522 1999 5

Photographs © Jamie Budge and Jack Gould, 2001.

9 8 7 6 5 4 3 2 1

A CIP catalogue record for this book is available from the British Library.

Design and typesetting by Jane Coney
Colour reproduction by Aylesbury Studios Ltd
Printed by New Interlitho

This book accompanies the television programme
Scrapheap Challenge,
made by RDF Media for Channel 4.
Executive Producer/Co-Presenter: Cathy Rogers
Series Producer: Jeremy Cross
Production Supervisor: Peter Clews

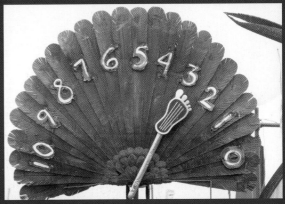

FOR CATHY ROGERS,
FOR WITHOUT HER,
NONE OF THIS WOULD
HAVE BEEN NECESSARY.

CONTENTS

SCRAPHEAP CHALLENGE

Once you're right in the middle of something chaotic and all-engulfing, like a noisy, dirty production day on *Scrapheap Challenge*, it's very difficult to go back in time and work out how on earth it all started.

It could be that I got involved in *Scrapheap* because when I was about eleven, I built a three-speed gearbox and a rack and pinion steering system out of Meccano. I even tried my hand at building independent suspension on a four-wheel drive model Meccano car, but I ran out of parts. I only had two universal coupling units, and although I tried constructing more out of small parts, the whole project ground to a halt. I've got to admit I fear a repeat of this if I ever take part as a team member in the show: 'Oh, we can't find a bit to do that job. Well, that's it then, isn't it. I'll give up now.'

It could even be that although I'm a total wimp, I can change wheels, spark plugs, even gearboxes on cars when really pressured to do so. Well, on old cars. New ones leave me a bit baffled. I have a basic understanding of the internal combustion engine, I know why planes fly and boats float, I can give a pretty good impression of describing how a jet engine works and I nearly understand helicopters.

'HOUSTON, WE HAVE A PROBLEM.'

Of course this has nothing to do with the show, or why it exists. For the record it actually all started when Cathy Rogers, the creator, executive producer and co-presenter of the show saw the movie *Apollo 13*.

'Houston, we have a problem,' says Tom Hanks. They have a power failure and are going to suffocate if someone back on earth doesn't do something clever to save them. Not something brave and action-packed, not charging in with a gun and blowing away the badly cast baddies. Something clever. The scientists on the ground work out that they could make an oxygen scrubber using materials they know the crew have on board. Bits of tubing, electric motors, fans, old strips of cloth, all held together with duct tape. They talk the endangered crew through what they have to do and eventually save their lives.

This intrigued Cathy and fellow producer Eve Kay, who had also seen the movie. During a meeting with David Frank, the co-founder of RDF Media, the company that makes *Scrapheap Challenge*, they reached their 'Eureka!' moment.

'We could recreate moments from history when people devised ingenious things to solve problems – like the one on *Apollo 13*. We could get John Blashford Snell to present it.'

'Yeah, yeah, we could actually get them to make what the scientists made.'

Robert Llewellyn, April 2001.

'Of course, the scientists in Houston only had what the crew of the ship had thrown away.'

'Thrown away – trash. They'd have to make something out of rubbish.'

'Making stuff out of scrap… we could do it on a scrapheap. How about a team of engineers on a scrapheap who have to make something out of what they can find?'

'Not an actual recreation from history?'

'Not necessarily. Just different engineering problems. And they have to do it in a set time limit.'

'We could call it *Scrapheap*.'

Cathy started talking it over with the people who would soon become the backbone of the *Scrapheap* series. For weeks, they kicked around different takes on the idea. They thought about trapping a scientist in a remote location, like up one of those enormously tall cranes that decorate the London skyline. This scientist would then have to guide a team of engineers who were running around a scrapyard hundreds of feet below to make some complex machine. This developed into the idea that the experts would join a team of three engineers, and their progress would be assessed by a judge – a specialist in the field.

'WE COULD CALL IT SCRAPHEAP'

Eventually Channel 4 commissioned a pilot, a one-off programme where two

Mad Max – Muggins himself in Series One.

teams of engineers – with their specialist helping them, not stuck up a crane – had to build a hovercraft in one day using the stuff they found on a giant scrap-yard in Bristol.

I didn't have anything to do with it, and I didn't even see it when it was broadcast, although I later found out that a lot of people did. I was sent a tape and I thought it looked interesting. I love the idea of making things, even if I'm pretty rubbish at doing it myself.

So, a little while later I sat down in a funny little office on Fulham Broadway in London and I met a group of people, including this enthusiastic woman called Cathy Rogers, who told me about this series they'd been commissioned to make, called *Scrapheap*.

I wasn't sure about getting involved when I first heard about it. I'm not crazy about the whole game show thing. In particular, I find 'makeover shows' a bit... well, I don't want to be overly critical. Oh, all right, I can't bloody stand them, watching a know-all smug presenter of either gender rip someone's home apart then glue a repugnant piece of MDF over the top of a window, cover it in fake zebra skin and arrange bits of twisted willow below it. Or build endless decking in endless suburban back gardens. I know these shows are popular, I know everyone loves them, but they leave me cold. No, I really didn't want to go anywhere near it. Don't get me wrong, I've done some cheap gigs, but even I have standards.

You see, I can't stand TV presenters. People with nice teeth and naff hair who talk... in that special... way directly to... camera. Real people never talk like that to each other in everyday life, it's like a new language that I firmly believe started in Australia. I have nothing to prove this theory other than the fact that you'd be amazed how many of our top radio DJs over the last forty years have been Australian. The job of a radio DJ is, I suppose, to fill the air between the music so that no one tunes in to another station. I believe they learn to do some sort of special circular breathing technique based on how you play the didgeridoo. It must be an Aboriginal cultural influence that white Australians are still in denial about. These people don't leave any gaps between sentences, they take breaths in the middle of phrases where no other English speaker would... huh... dream of taking... huh... a breath. TV

WOULD I BECOME ONE OF THESE PEOPLE WITHOUT REALIZING IT? WOULD MY HAIR SUDDENLY GO FLUFFY? WOULD I START WORRYING ABOUT WHAT I WORE?

presenters seem to have followed the trend, and it has become the norm.

So all these things were rattling about in my brain as I caught the Tube home from meeting Cathy and the fledgling *Scrapheap* crew. Would I become one of these people without realizing it? Would my hair suddenly go fluffy? Would I start worrying about what I wore? Having been in a sit-com for the previous ten years in which I was completely covered in rubber and plastic, I'd been partially protected from brutal B-list micro-celebrity recognition and its concomitant neurosis.

Looking back now, on my way to Los Angeles, California, to record the fourth series of *Scrapheap Challenge*, I know I was being a complete tosser. No one is interested in who presents the show. It's not about some poncy presenters and their minor career worries, it's about a group of people the telly has chosen, up until recently, to ignore. *Scrapheap Challenge* is about people who can invent things, make things, fix things that look utterly knackered and beyond repair. It's about people whose brains don't give up when faced with a difficult technical problem. Over the four series, I've become increasingly aware of the huge skill pool we have in the UK that often lies unused. For all our failings, bad practice, pollution, lazy management and blame-obsessed culture, we're still really good at making stuff.

We used to be world leaders, of course – ships, planes, cars, trains. I recently discovered we sold over 200,000 Morris Minors in America in the fifties. Imagine that: a Morris Minor going down Park Avenue, New York, or even Sunset Boulevard. Doesn't seem possible, does it?

Our bridges spanned the world's rivers, our trains ran on tracks in over forty

Bowser, Chen and Anne from Series One...

countries, our ships sailed everywhere, our planes flew even further. They were all made in this country by people like Bowser, Colonel Dick, Spike and Nosher. People who worked stuff out, drew designs in chalk on dirty workbenches, cut bits of metal and joined them together and built things.

OK, so now it's really only top-quality tanks and guided missile systems that we produce in any great number. Oh, and small arms and explosives, landmines and anti-personnel grenades, vertical take-off fighters and attack helicopters. We're really good at making all those sorts of things, which is fine. It's just a shame that they seem to be virtually all we produce now.

So a few weeks after my first meeting, I turned up at a scrapyard in Brentford, just off the M4 flyover. It was all very exciting and different, and it clearly wasn't a garden makeover show. As I read through what the teams were supposed to do, it appeared at first to be completely impossible. I couldn't understand how these two teams of very different individuals could possibly make anything so complicated in one day. But they did.

In the first series, the teams remained the same throughout all six programmes. Anne headed one team with Bowser and Chen. The other team was led by Major (later Colonel) Dick, with team members Dave and Kali. Each week they'd be joined by a different specialist with experience in the area. Boat-builders, power-pulling champions, medieval siege engine experts, deep-sea diving instructors and people I didn't even know existed turned up at the scrapyard in Brentford. The teams faced six different challenges: sub-aqua, in the shape of a diving bell; power-pullers, a sort of mad tractor tug of war; flinging turnips and cabbages with medieval siege engines; a powerboat challenge; an off-road buggy race held at three in the morning; and finally, shooting a snow-scene toy into space on top of a cardboard tube rocket, and theoretically bringing it safely to earth.

It was great fun to do, one of those weird Channel 4 shows that goes out on Sundays and no one sees; at least, that's what I expected it to be. By the end of it, we seemed to have done just about everything we could do and that was it. I watched it with my kids, and my five year-old son loved it. He built a wonderful little siege engine out of plastic Duplo bricks, powered by a rubber band. A proud moment for a dad – I watched him carefully as he sat on the floor working it out. It was a mini *Scrapheap* experience, but more importantly it was the first time I'd seen him try to recreate something he'd seen on telly. It felt like the show was a bit more important than I had originally given it credit for.

I went on and did another series of *Red Dwarf* and sort of forgot about the whole *Heap* thing. Then Cathy rang me one day and said that the viewing figures were really good and that

... And their sworn foes Dick, Dave and Kali.

Channel 4 wanted us to make another series. Just to put this into context, I have done enough series, programmes, pilots, readings and scripts that were never broadcast, let alone made it to a second series, to know what a small chance there is of this happening. I was pleased and very surprised.

Second time around, the *Scrapheap* location was in Canning Town, bigger and dirtier than Brentford, but better organized. This time it was a knockout contest. Different teams took part each week and the winners of each round went up through the competition to the grand final. The challenges were extraordinary and the teams were amazingly variable in terms of technical skill, but all so completely committed.

The other different thing about the second series was that I was joined on screen by Cathy, which was a great idea and how it should have been from the start. I'd quite like to be a bitter TV presenter, who'd thrown a big wobbly and huffed off the set because the broadcasters clearly didn't think I could do the job on my own and had to bring in 'some woman' to keep the audience watching; I'd have got more attention. But then before I knew it I'd have been demanding a stretch limo to take me to the shops and I'd... huh... be speaking like... huh... this all the... huh... time. The truth of the matter is that Cathy and I have become close friends through the show and I find working with her a joy. In real life she is a very clever, very beautiful, very happy and extraordinarily funny, foul-mouthed woman. In fact, I hate her. She makes me sick, everyone likes her, everyone says how clever she is, how beautiful, she makes me sick sick sick.

Enough about her already.

The second series was when the show really took off. Having new teams each week gave it a new level of energy and

Robert was joined by a professional at last for Series Two.

urgency. We really didn't know who was going to win. There was a lot of backstage betting – like on whose cannon was going to work and whose would blow up and destroy the mini-cam. Invariably we were wrong, but Sim and Richard, the backstage technical crew on Series Two and Three, had an uncanny ability to predict who would win.

THE DAY IS LONG, HARD AND DIRTY

To the casual passer-by, Sim and Richard could look quite threatening, a couple of grease-caked oil-voles who would sell you your own car before you knew what was happening. But they could 'source' weird bits of mechanical kit that ordinary mortals wouldn't have heard of, and they could do it with apparently little effort. They could also start the most recalcitrant engine when the teams had been fiddling with it for hours.

This is something I have learned through watching the teams struggle with their creations. If the challenge involves an engine of any sort, be it for a giant mower or a motorboat, one thing you can always rely on is that it won't start. If someone could be bothered to analyze the amount of time team members spent fiddling with engines, it would take up an uncomfortable percentage of their day. A lot of people, like me, understand the mechanical rudiments of the internal combustion engine but, also like me, haven't got a clue about the electrics. And it's always the electrics that are at fault. Thankfully for all concerned, Sim and Richard would appear at the eleventh hour, which is worrying when the teams only have ten hours to build their creations. They would discreetly join a couple of wires, hit something with a hammer, mutter obscenities under their breaths and the engine would burst into life.

Don't get me wrong – it's not as though there's a gang of people behind the scenes ready to help the teams at any moment. The teams have to really suffer before an outsider steps in, but if it's becoming obvious that they don't have a hope of completing the challenge because of a minor engine problem, the oil-voles are there to give a hand. If this seems in any way to diminish the utter dedication and skill of the teams, then I've given the wrong impression. I have yet to be un-amazed by the level of enthusiasm displayed by the participants of *Scrapheap*, even when they know what they are in for.

The day is long, hard and dirty. We start at about 5.30am and often don't finish until 10.30pm. During that time, everyone involved in the show – apart from the teams – has the odd rest. Even me. The camera crews work in shifts, even the director will get time to sit down and take it easy for a couple of minutes, but the teams are searching and building for every second, other than when we actually force them to have lunch. And we do insist on a compulsory one-hour break for lunch to make sure they eat something. If we didn't, they'd be eating their lunch as they cut through sheet steel with an oxy torch, or ground down the end of an axle that, with a lot of hassle, might just be the right length.

We turn off the cameras and leave them in peace for a bit. Nine times out of ten, they talk about the project in hand. Of course, even though they're not on camera, we can still hear everything they say. Cathy and I, along with the director

The Series Two finale, after a hard day testing the slowest machines ever made of scrap.

and half the crew, are wearing earpieces that relay us their discussions so we don't miss anything. As the whole programme is shot on the fly, we have to be ready to move at any second of the day if something amazing or terrible happens. Cathy and I greet either occurrence with equal enthusiasm; when something starts to work – a problematic engine, say – we rush into the build area and check it out. But if something goes wrong – a fire, a massive collapse of a much-fought-over structure – great, a total disaster! – in we go to check it out again.

The brave teams in Series Two faced building an amphibious vehicle, a cannon, a flying machine, a high-mileage vehicle, a land yacht, a marine salvage crane and, finally and insanely, a walking machine.

Eventually, after triumph and heartache, Series Two was in the can. We had done it again, seven programmes had been shot, and everyone was utterly exhausted. Even fit young men who had buckets of energy at the beginning of the series could be found lying in heaps in the backs of vans. There were stories of members of the crew who had woken up late, sitting on their sofas at home with a cold bowl of soup on their laps. They had simply collapsed the night before and lost the ability to eat.

Still, I thought, two series, not bad, made some really amazing machines, went to some really weird locations, met some brilliant people. But that was it, game over, man. These sorts of things never last that long.

Early the following year, Cathy rang me again: 'They want another series Robert! What are we going to do?'

'A windmill?' I half-suggested.

And a windmill it was that I watched turn slowly in the drizzle of a spring day three months later. We were on Beachy Head – according to local legend, the windiest place in England. The windiest place in England until we got there. It was utterly still and very wet, but the windmills sort of worked eventually, grinding up some very lumpy, damp coffee. The windmill challenge in Series Three still holds the record for being the wettest one we have ever undertaken.

In Series Three, everything was even bigger, more challenging, more explosive,

Series Three: two top professionals... at least you can't quite see the tie.

deeper, higher and harder. For the first time, I went along to a couple of the preliminary meetings where the challenges are decided upon. I tried to sit quietly and let the frighteningly bright team that's behind the show come out with their ideas first, but of course my big mouth opened and half a dozen half-baked, unfocused ideas tumbled out:

'What about a re-entry vehicle, a twin-rotor helicopter, a pair of high-powered rocket pants?'

Frozen faces around the table. Only Cathy at the other end gave a kind smile: 'Thank you, Robert... Now, moving on...'

I have never been involved in a show that has more pre-production planning. There are so many factors to consider when setting a challenge. Is it possible? Is it too dangerous? Is it just too plain silly? But all the rules, as viewers will know, have been broken many times.

In Series Three, the teams – some old favourites, some new and fresh-faced – had to create a giant mower, a bridging machine, an aerial bomber, a demolition machine, a fireboat, a human-powered cannon, an underwater chariot, a windmill, a steam car and, finally, a dragster.

We had more adventures during the production. Highs, like the time the entire crew ended up in a huge heated swimming pool on one of those very rare, for England, warm summer evenings; lows, like the time we arrived at a chalk pit in Luton at 3.00am to film the aerial bombers. The plan was that only at dawn would the air be still enough to fly the giant airship; of course, as it turned out, it was seven hours later before the wind even thought about calming down.

Spud, another great behind-the-scenes *Scrapheap* character, reached his lowest point that morning. Spud is a wonderfully avuncular Australian who keeps the many cameras the show requires in tip-top order. He has a massive knowledge of all things technical and suffers from hay fever.

When we're on a difficult location, like the Luton chalk pit, we use the quad bikes to get equipment around. Spud had been roaring around carrying camera

IS IT POSSIBLE? IS IT TOO DANGEROUS? IS IT JUST TOO PLAIN SILLY?

operators and their equipment to their positions since 3.00am. Just as we started to shoot a sequence, we heard a horn blast out. A quick scan of the horizon and we located the source. It was Spud, his helmeted head resting on the horn of a quad bike. He had finally fallen asleep on the job, eyes swollen with hay fever, looking, it has to be said, rougher than the rest of us, which is in the realms of extreme roughness.

In Series Three we actually had a big finale with an audience – the drag race, where the Brothers in Arms used the axle from an old Post Office truck, welded on to a botched-together chassis and powered by a Rover V8 engine that had seen better days, to go up against the Megalomaniacs' motorbike trike, which featured some very slick engineering. The event was held on a drag strip in Warwickshire and a large crowd of fans, friends and families of the teams turned up to witness the race. They saw first-hand the amazing spectacle of Colonel Richard Strawbridge driving their scrap-built dragster backwards at 40 miles an hour – forced to do so by the total lack of any forward gears. They also saw the crown princes of trash, the great Nosher and his Megalomaniac team, proudly hold up the scrap trophy as the all-time champions of the show.

Beauty and the beast, Series Four.

So that was it. Three series and I had actually started to notice the popularity of the show in my daily life. People would come up to me in the supermarket and tell me how much they loved the

I ALWAYS FEEL A LITTLE BIT GUILTY BECAUSE I DIDN'T MAKE ANYTHING, I JUST WATCHED.

show, a very nice tribute although I always feel a little bit guilty because I didn't make anything, I just watched.

Life took over again, until I had a call from Cathy.

'HOW WOULD YOU FEEL ABOUT MAKING ANOTHER SERIES IN LOS ANGELES?'

GIANT EGG SHOOTER

Early morning. I rush along the already busy Los Angeles freeway system towards the location for *Scrapheap Challenge* Series Four. By autumn 2000, the three previous series of *Scrapheap* had been shown by an American broadcaster called The Learning Channel (TLC), and it had proved very successful. The company behind the show, RDF Media, had been commissioned to make an American version, *Junkyard Wars*, with an American presenter, George Gray, alongside Cathy. The show had been made in England, but featured American teams who were flown over to the UK to take part.

I was called back in to co-host the grand final of finals, where the *Scrapheap Challenge* winners in the form of the Megalomaniacs faced the *Junkyard Wars* finalists, the Long Brothers. The Americans won, but the show was, as they say in America, 'a blast', featuring 'awesome' car-flattening machines.

Series Four is filmed in California, with English teams flown out to America to take part. Three-quarters of the behind-the-scenes crew are already settled in West Hollywood by the time I arrive. A day after I stumble off the plane, the first teams land at LAX and are swished to their luxury apartments in huge stretch limos… Oh, all right, they're living in small apartments on the wrong side of the tracks and they all have to squash into the back of a small and rather grubby Honda. This is *Scrapheap*, after all.

I don't see the new set for the show until two days before we record the first build, but when I get there, it's a bit overwhelming. For a start, it's not the sort of place most people imagine when they think of 'Hollywood'. It's surrounded on all sides by thousands of acres of landfill sites, concrete-crushing plants and mile after mile of piled-up discarded vehicles. For people who aren't as *au fait* with the whole Hollywood thing as a media giant like me, I'll explain. The city of Los Angeles is pretty big in that it takes about an hour to fly over it in a 747. Big in that it's bigger than anything else created by the human race. It's huge, it goes on forever and it has

THIS IS SCRAPHEAP AFTER ALL

no middle bit. Running east–west across the centre is a range of hills, one side of which sports that famous white sign. On the southern side are all those places we've heard of, Beverly Hills, Hollywood, Santa Monica, Venice Beach and all that. On the northern side of the hills is what is known locally as 'the valley'. The San Fernando valley is, I suppose, a valley in that it is surrounded by hills and mountains, but it's a bit big by my definition. You could easily drive for an hour in any direction and not come to the edge. Sun Valley is a suburb within this massive flat sprawl. 'Sun Valley' sounds so sweet and rural, with rolling hills and cows munching lush grass… in fact, it's a vast industrial wasteland and therefore, obviously, the location for the series.

Hard at work.

The set is fantastic, and the new Scrapmobile is just brilliant; Annabel Mazzotti, the designer, has done herself proud. She has built the settings for all the *Scrapheap* series but this is the most ambitious. She has shipped two container-loads of British scrap to California, which has to be one of the least expected exports to leave our shores. In amongst piled-up Chevrolets and Oldsmobiles is an old London taxi, a Mini, a couple of MG sports cars, numerous motorbikes and all manner of decorative rubbish that Annabel turns into things of great beauty.

Cathy and I do a photo shoot with an American photographer, which ends with us hanging precariously from an overhanging beam. I wander around in a bit of a jet-lagged haze trying to take in the enormous amount of organization that has gone into turning an American junkyard into the setting for the new series. I know the researchers spent weeks looking for a suitable location, checking out junkyards over a huge area. The one they've finally chosen is called Memory Lane, as it contains thousands of 'classic period cars', those great slabs of Detroit steel with wings on the back, massive engines and petrol consumption to be proud of.

Jeremy Cross, our insanely enthusiastic producer since Series Three, is rushing around in a frenzy of delight: 'Bobby, Bobby, come and look at this!'

He shows me an old hearse crushed under a London taxi. He's clearly having a lot of fun. He explains some of the differences between London and LA that the crew have been experiencing. In London, if we need a load of old rope or some heavy steel box section, it might cost a couple of quid but basically, as it's lying around getting in the way, most scrappies aren't that bothered about it. In fact, if they've heard of the show they're usually more than helpful, bit of a story to tell down the pub. But now we're working in the movie capital of the world where everything has a value. Everyone knows how the movie and TV industry works here; they know everything about how it's set up even if they aren't employed by it directly. Finding someone in LA who isn't in some way connected to the movies is very hard. This isn't to say that the locals aren't helpful; they are, and incredibly supportive. But there is a cultural divide and it's clearly taken a little time for the British crew to find their way.

'Is it the 101 all the way?' asks Cathy at 5.30am on the first day. We're driving along Highway 101, and I am attempting to look at the map, but I'm not being much help: 'Think so.'

Cathy sees something she recognizes and we pull off the eight-lane monster on to a boulevard, an LA side-street the width of the Champs Elysées. On to another dusty street, then a left down an even dustier one that's just massive trucks, huge concrete walls and big steel gates – the sort of place that's used when Mel Gibson has to save the girl in *Lethal Weapon 7*.

Suddenly, we see a pool of light and actual people milling around. There's Spud and Jeremy, and loads of new people I've never seen before. It's still dark but it's busy as hell. It seems like hundreds of people are milling about, carrying lights, cameras, bits of wire, or in my case a coffee cup. The new people are all American and really friendly, but already the American way of doing things is apparent. In England I receive no special treatment because I appear on camera, far from it. But in America, he who appears on screen is touched by God.

'What would you like for breakfast, Robert?'

'Oh, blimey, what is there?'

Fatal response in America. The choice you are faced with when it comes to food can take an hour to listen to. I stop Andrew (the charming second assistant director) halfway through, and choose an omelette. In Canning Town I get my own breakfast, but it seems that's out of the question here.

Eloise Robinson has made the costumes Cathy and I wear for every series. She also makes and converts the teams' workwear, makes sure they've all got boots, tool belts, gloves, knee-pads, helmets and sun cream. Eloise is always a little busy at the start of the day, but her Portacabin is where I head first. It's a little haven of sanity in an otherwise dark, chaotic and bustling world.

I have a new costume for the new series, and I like it. It's light and comfortable, it's not a white suit and I'm not wearing a huge kipper tie. It's odd what people who

Admiring the new costumes.

watch the show will pick up on. I met quite a few people when Series Three was being broadcast who just said 'Tie', and not in a nice way.

One of the great things about *Scrapheap* is the early morning stumble when we meet the teams. When I meet them for the first time, the two teams taking part in the first recording are clearly a little wibbly-wobbly from jetlag. However, the excitement of being able to 'have a go' on *Scrapheap* means they're feeling very chipper. They are Storm Force, three lifeboat men from Dorset, and the Dirty Dancers, three engineers who met at ballroom dancing classes. Excellent.

There is always a lot of bonhomie and jocularity as people slowly change into their team colours and get 'commed up', as it's referred to, where the sound crew fit the teams with radio microphones and walkie-talkies, so they can talk to each other and we can listen in.

Cathy and I are guided by the complex hierarchy of American production staff on to the set as the sun starts to climb over the distant San Raphael mountains.

'Welcome to *Scrapheap Challenge*...'

C-C-California c-c-can be c-c-cold: Storm Force and the Dirty Dancers

We've actually started. I've travelled three-quarters of the way around the world to be here, from Sydney where I've been living with my family, to London for ten days, then to LA. I'm a bit confused, but as soon as Gerard (first assistant director) says 'action', it all feels OK again.

In many ways this is the most painful and frustrating period for the teams. They have applied to be on the show because they want to have a go at building something; so once they are in their overalls, with their helmets on and their comms fitted, they are busting to get stuck in. But due to the vagaries of television production, there are always hundreds of little things that need to be sorted out before we can allow them to start.

As this is the first programme we have ever made in the USA, it's even more chaotic than usual. Add this to the fact that they really don't know what they're going to be asked to do and you can sense the pressure they're under.

Eventually they are gathered before myself and Cathy, and we reveal the challenge. The Dirty Dancers and Storm Force have to build a machine that can

GENUINE SHOCK AND BEWILDERMENT

project an ostrich egg over the greatest distance possible, without breaking it. Gratifyingly, they react to this information with quite genuine shock and bewilderment, but they have to go through even this opening routine three or four times for the director to get all the camera angles needed.

However, once we finally set them going, they keep going, no matter what. The teams really do build the machines in one day, and once they start, they work incredibly hard. If you're sitting still doing nothing, ten hours can seem like forever; but if you have to build a large, complex machine with lots of components that could easily fail, it's amazing how fast the hours pass.

A few days before the shoot, a local ostrich farm supplied us with two dozen eggs. Ostrich eggs are heavy and they can break... It's an insane challenge – I look at an egg, of course it's going to break. Whose daft idea was it?

After the initial planning stage in which the team experts suggest their plans, the scavengers roar off on their six-wheeled all-terrain buggies to collect what they need. Richard, the 6'5" scavenger for the Storm Force team, has trouble driving the little monster. He's so big, he can't pull the lever back far enough to stop the damn thing. It doesn't have a steering wheel or handlebars like the quads we have used in the past. You drive it like a tank: two levers – both forward and you go forward; pull one back you turn left or right; pull both back, you stop. Richard just can't pull them back, and within the first five minutes of the contest he's crashed it ten times. Not badly,

The start of the challenge, with much stylish running in evidence as usual.

you understand, he just gently ploughs into things saying, 'How do you stop this bloody thing?'

Storm Force have Paul Denny as an expert, who we've met before on the show. He is the country's only medieval siege engine maintenance expert; I suppose it's just as well there aren't hordes of them around, as there might not be enough medieval siege engines to keep them all busy. He has suggested they use a 2000 year-old Greek design, a sort of giant four-poster bed frame with twisted rope on each side into which two big spars of wood are inserted and twisted, giving it enormous twisty flicking power. The ostrich egg is to be housed in a sort of padded missile that will be shot out, Paul estimates, at about 100 miles an hour. They will fit a little parachute on to the missile to slow it down before it lands, in an attempt to avoid serious ostrich egg scramblage.

The Dirty Dancers have Jem Stansfield who, as far as I can tell, is completely

Using a high-tech method of checking the egg launch rails are true.

barking mad, in the nicest possible way. He can drink two pints of beer while standing on his head. He can do it so fast he holds the world record. He also holds a record in Australia for long-distance egg-catching. I'm sure he can do a lot of other things, but when you hear about this particular skill you don't like to ask. Jem's plan, which the Dirty Dancers seize upon with glee, is to build a totally insane machine that uses a motorbike, a long bit of string and a huge framework that will launch the hapless ostrich egg into orbit. I listen to them working out how to do it, and a little while later, director Jane Tweddle asks me what I think their plan is.

'It's a motorbike-powered launchy thing with string and a big shooty thing that's got a thing in it that goes along, and the egg is in that – and a little hook comes undone and the egg keeps going, I think.' This is about the best I can do. Jane smiles and goes to look for someone who understands.

I am relieved that at last the teams are building something, but the day seems to have started very slowly. In a brief quiet moment Cathy and I try to work out why it feels so different. We have each interviewed one of the teams and it all seems very normal, in an insane *Scrapheap* sort of way. It hasn't been too hard and that worries me; I always feel nervous when something has gone well and everybody says, 'That was really, really OK.' For some reason, it should be harder. What if we're being too glib, or too presenter-ish? It's very difficult to judge, and we just have to trust the production team.

Yes, Robert, you can have one for lunch.

However, our confusion pales into insignificance when I see how Richard, the man in control of the sound department, and Spud, on cameras, are both flying around like headless chickens. Nothing goes wrong that can't be put right, but hundreds of new small problems have to be dealt with.

Richard has come over to help the American sound crew understand the odd way of working we've developed. Everything is slightly different; sometimes better, sometimes worse. When we worked in Canning Town, I would wear an earpiece that could tune into the teams' channel so I could hear what was going on. However, very often I would hear a crane operator on a local building site berate his colleagues with what can only be described as colourful language. This was amusing the first couple of times, but when yet another obscene tirade about a pile of sand in the wrong place interrupted an important bit of information I was trying to get, it began to drive me potty.

No such problem in America. I can hear the teams with crystal clarity; there's no interference. However, my own microphone is apparently going click click all the time, making recording my voice impossible. I feel a bit guilty, even though I know

And the egg will fit safely in here... yeah, right.

it's not my fault. I always like to feel guilty about something. In between takes, the patient sound man changes the battery, the mic cover, the wire, the whole set-up, but still there are little click click sounds every time I move.

After a lot of experimenting, Spud and Richard decide it's my waistcoat, made especially by costume supremo Eloise Robinson. The material has metal strips in it that are shorting out the transmitter pack. Now Eloise feels guilty, but it's not her fault either; it's just one of those myriad problems you could never foresee. They stick the transmitter in a leather pouch and hang it off my belt. Problem solved.

Both teams have found what looks to be a rather alarming amount of very new-looking steel box section, which they are busy cutting and welding. Viewers often ask us whether the stuff on *Scrapheap* is 'planted' by us. Nine times out of ten it isn't. The teams find whatever they can on the yard, and use that. When there is a very specific safety issue, like using non-return valves for a diving bell, or a steam engine that has to have passed a safety test, these things are left hidden on the heap by the wily and brutally fair technical crew.

However, this is the first of a new series, and the new head of the engineering department (a charming German fellow called Tristan Chytroschek who bears an uncanny resemblance to Woody in *Toy Story*) has 'seeded' about three times more steel box section than is polite. What

IT LOOKS LIKE A FIFTIES SCI-FI MOON ROCKET LAUNCHER

happened was that Tristan ordered enough box section for the whole series, but instead of stashing it off the set, he piled the whole lot up behind an old van. And what did the teams do when they found it? They went, 'Yahoo! Treasure trove!'

Weeks before any of the teams arrive, the experts speak to the researchers and say something like, 'To build a 2000 year-old Greek siege engine, I really need a whole bunch of steel box section.' The researchers reply along the lines of, 'We'll see what we can do,' which in *Scrap* code means, 'Yeah, right, as if!' Normally, if there was any potential danger in building a machine that didn't have a bit of strong box section steel to reinforce some vital area, then enough would be planted – but not a whole truckload. Somehow, in the new set-up, the message got scrambled.

THIS IS FRATERNIZING WITH THE ENEMY

But the teams are delighted. Being skilled metalworkers, the Storm Force crew have welded together a giant steel four-poster bed before lunch. They are sailing through the build. On the Dirty Dancer side, there is a pile of steel and a motorbike with no front wheel and an engine that won't start. I'm beginning to feel more at home.

We break for lunch, the teams stand down and their lunch is delivered to them on the set. The crew retire to the dust-blown street and feast on a massive spread supplied by the Cockney catering company. Again, a strange feeling, being in America but having lunch cooked by a bunch of diamond geezers who would blend perfectly into a Canning Town setting. When we return to the set, it all feels very different – the teams are sitting together chatting and joking about what they are building. There's nothing wrong with this, but it's never happened before; we like to keep the teams apart and keep them guessing about what the other one's up to. Of course they all devise devious ways of finding out, but not like this – this is fraternizing with the enemy and it feels as though the show has gone a bit sloppy. I can tell Cathy is upset. The show is her baby, after all; the way it's run has developed over three years and this isn't part of it. The teams are very good-natured and soon set back to work, but it's thrown us all a bit.

As the weak sun starts to head west, both teams' machines are taking shape. The Storm Force creation is making more sense as it nears completion, while the Dirty Dancers' humungous structure makes less and less. It looks like a fifties sci-fi moon rocket launcher, but I start to get convinced that it might just work.

By the time we approach the ten-hour build limit, and everyone is cold and tired, I confer with Cathy. We have both cheered up, we're both tired, the teams seem to

IT FEELS LIKE IT'S BACK TO NORMAL

be taking an age to finish, it's cold, dark and there's the smell of rain in the air. We could easily be in Canning Town and agree that this is how *Scrapheap* should be. It feels like it's back to normal.

The Dirty Dancers' 900cc motorbike engine roars into life, spinning the flywheel that will wind in a piece of string at 100mph and launch their enormously heavy missile with its egg payload. Storm Force start to crank up their twisty rope launcher and Cathy can't look. She has a problem with twisty rope machines, always has. I don't know if she can get help with twisty rope phobia but I make

Shocking proof that the teams do actually get on.

a mental note to check it out on the internet.

I finally call the build to a halt and the teams cheer as best they can, but they are clearly exhausted. They are all still suffering a little from jetlag and the classic *Scrapheap Challenge* problem of staying up rather late the night before, consuming quantities of fermented vegetable drinks. I am always impressed at how they do this, as I have to go to bed early with a cup of cocoa and one of the classics propped on my lap.

We stumble around in the dark again, just as we did when we arrived, handing back the mass of sound equipment we are all festooned with. Everyone wants to get home and into a bath, which I manage to do before midnight – pretty good going on *Scrappers*.

GIANT EGG SHOOTER

The Test

Cathy is talking to her sister in London as we speed up Highway 101 at 5.45am. It's the test day for the giant egg shooters, which is taking place on a large open site near one of Los Angeles' many enormous reservoirs. Building a massive city in what is effectively a desert brings with it a series of special problems, the primary one being water (the movie *Chinatown* chronicled the rather murky history of how the city procured its supply, if you're interested).

The Dirty Dancers looking chipper.

I have a map on my lap, but I'm just looking at the range of mountains before us, their tops obscured by clouds. We are supposed to take the 118 and go along Ronald Reagan Boulevard, but suddenly I see a sign for the 121. A quick glance at the map confirms that I have screwed up.

'Roberto!' wails Cathy. It's all my fault, and although I consider muttering something about her being on the phone while she drives, I keep shtum. We would have been nice and early, had time to have

Storm Force looking butch.

breakfast and take a couple of minutes to get prepared. As it is, we turn around and join the morning rush hour traffic back into LA. It's staggering how many cars there are. Even when you're used to England and the choking motorways, these are just bigger and more choked with bigger cars, all with one person in them.

Once we find the site, we get changed and eat on the run, and before long I stand on top of a pile of huge boulders to introduce the test. I check the picture on the little monitor that's mounted on the large camera crane and try to work out why even a picture on a TV screen looks 'bigger' in America. Maybe it's to do with the

Cathy inspects the terror that's about to be unleashed.

sky, the sheer size of the place and the light. I'm not sure, but it looks very different to someone standing on top of a pile of old rocks in England.

The location is a huge slab of gritty wasteland to the rear of a newly built dam. There is certainly plenty of room to fire the eggs. Two *Scrapheap* old-timers, Ian and Dom, are spinning around on the newly acquired six-wheeler ATVs (all terrain vehicles to you, and me for that matter). I'd never seen the like before, except on the seventies kids' TV show *Banana Splits*. Ian and Dom exist in a bubble of boy heaven on the show. We just have to go on things like quad bikes, tanks, four-wheel drives, planes and weird boats. They both seem to know everything about leisure-based machinery, what sort of jet ski is the fastest, where to go bungee jumping, what sort of armour a certain tank is fitted with and how easy it is to turn a six-wheel ATV upside down. Dom discovered this the first day he used one, then did it again so that Ian could take a picture of it. Dom's screen saver on his office computer is a picture of him on a quad bike, jumping through the air at tremendous speed. But these guys aren't macho in the accepted sense of the word. They are very sensitive, bright, well-educated boys; just a little mad, in a nice way. They're young and I forgive them, I just make sure I never get a lift anywhere with them as they can make the most gentle-looking saloon car do things that are quite unpleasant when you're inside. Actually I am being very unfair on Ian – he is a much safer driver, a lot less wild; the yin to Dom's yang.

The teams are preparing their machines at one end of the missile range. It's 218 yards long and for once I feel the teams may achieve a launch of this scale. Once everything is in place, any normal mortal would think that they'd just fire them, someone would win, and then we'd all go home. It never happens like this, as there are always great lists of things that have to be organized by someone. I used to try and follow everything that was going on, but I soon learned that it's best to let people do what they're doing and keep out of the way.

While we stand around, Waggie, the captain of Storm Force, tells tales of being underwater in a submarine for three months at a time. He was in the Navy before becoming a lifeboat man with the RNLI, which is where all the team now work. I learned things about submarines that I'd never even thought about, like what you do with all your rubbish. You crush it in a giant hydraulic crusher and drop it on the seabed when no one's looking. Same with human waste. Apparently the worst maintenance job on board the submarine is when the sewage masher breaks down – someone has to fix it. Everyone loves stories like that, and most of the people on both teams could probably fix a sewage masher on a submarine if they had to.

Somehow the conversation moves on to drinking and Jem, the expert on the Dirty Dancers team, tells us about his youth in Telford. How he got punched by a very large man in a pub when he was seventeen and how grateful he was that the man used his fist and not a glass. He explains there was a rash of 'glassings' going on in the town at the time. Being a wet liberal, I am glad to see the teams seem very shocked by this. Engineering types are very non-violent on the whole; although they can look quite menacing when fully oiled up, they are gentle souls who love to make things rather than destroy them. They discuss the prevalence of shell suits in the eighties; Shaun from the Dirty Dancers talks about Basildon in Essex, and the high shell suit density there. As we stand around fat-chewing, it's hard to believe we are anywhere other than some windblown ex-industrial site in England. That is, until an American runner appears and asks us to go and

Robert inspects Jem for outward signs of madness.

start the challenge. I get offered a lift in a car. The start line is all of 50 metres from where I'm standing so I excuse myself, saying I need the exercise. I think Americans would drive to the bathroom if they could get their cars in their houses.

Storm Force prepare to fire first, winching back the two wooden arms that twist the burly skeins of rope. These act as the spring. It's twisty rope heaven, unless you're Cathy, but she's way down the other end of the firing range, ready to go and inspect the egg when it has landed. The missile is loaded into its trough, with the parachute they have made tucked into the rear. This is tied to a fishing line, which in turn is joined to a fishing rod held by team member Martin.

Waggie calls, 'Fire!'

Paul pulls the pin, and sproing! The giant wooden arms catapult the botched-together plastic projectile, which sails about 40 metres before Martin flicks the line and pulls out the parachute. The parachute doesn't open, of course – this is *Scrapheap* – and the missile lands with a sickening, egg-scrambling thud.

It actually works!

Moments later Cathy holds up a green flag. The egg is, amazingly, intact, and a cheer erupts from the Storm Force team. This means, by the unique rules of this challenge, that the Storm Force team move their launch contraption up the firing range to where their egg landed and prepare to fire again.

Now it is time for the Heath Robinson special. The Dirty Dancers load up their enormous heavy missile on its 45-degree launch chute, check their fishing rod line (they are using a similar parachute deployment system), fire up the 900cc motorbike, the rear tyre of which is resting on a small wheel, which is connected by an axle to a larger wheel, which winds in the string, which pulls the missile up the launch chute – and off into the heavens.

What's really incredible is that it works – but I don't know how or why. Anyone with any experience of how things go wrong, which I now consider myself to be something of an expert on, would say this daft machine was a sure-fire bet for disaster. Everyone stands in amazement as the missile is thrown high into the air. Even the parachute more or less deploys and the whole thing thumps into the ground.

Cath, stand a bit further back – you never know...

Again, Cathy and her team of *Scrap* scientists (actually Ian in a white coat) run up to the landing spot. It's a 'go' moment. Their red team flag goes up: the egg has survived, and the Dirty Dancers throw themselves about wildly. During all this commotion I sit in the back of the new Scrapmobile, a very battered ex-military Dodge pick-up, so it's all a bit distant. I'm sitting next to the judge on this challenge, Ivan Williams, a specialist in old weaponry who's also been on the show before. He's very much of the belief that Storm Force are going to win – they're using tried and trusted technology, even if it was tried and trusted 2000 years ago in Greece. However, he is mightily impressed by the Dirty Dancers' first launch.

This is very unlike *Scrapheap* – both teams have fired successfully and both eggs have landed without breaking. I worry that maybe we didn't make it hard enough. Maybe the teams are getting a bit too clever. However, my fears are put to rest after the second round, in which both eggs are smashed to bits, both machines suffer some damage and both missiles are crunched, bent and in dire need of maintenance. Excellent.

The Storm Force team repair and reload their egg-stained missile while the Dirty Dancers go off looking for twigs. On closer inspection it seems the Dancers are 'splinting up' their missile in an attempt to protect their egg for the third and final flight.

One after the other, both teams launch. It's genuinely neck-and-neck, too close to call. So who won?

That would be telling…

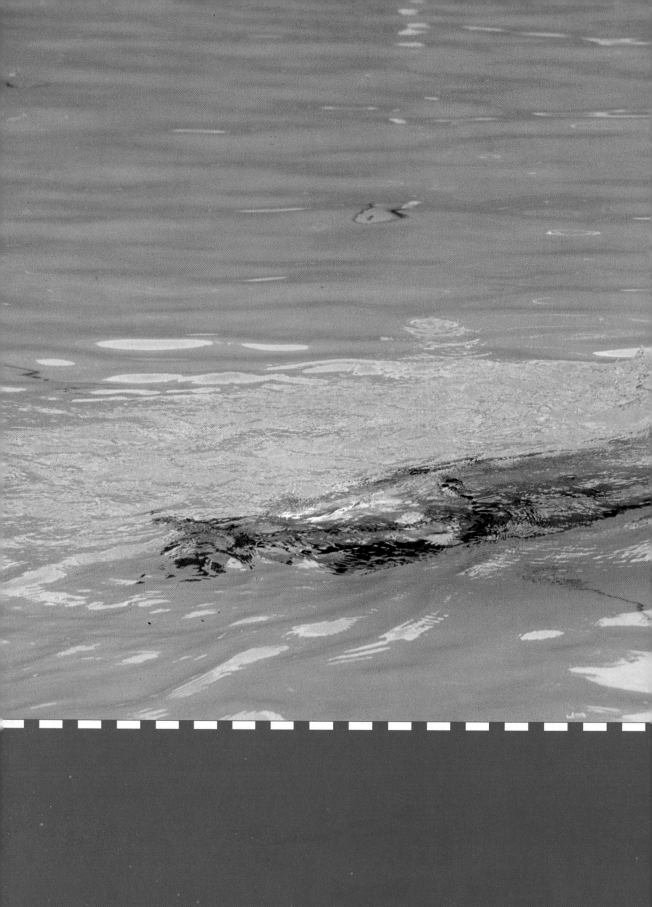

TORPEDO

At last, we see a sky that I consider to be the correct colour for the Southern Californian region. Bright blue, endless bright blue... and it's only 6.15am. Everything is different the second time I arrive at the site; it feels fresh, bright and totally Californian. Everything is in the right place, people know what they're doing and everyone seems happy. Especially the teams.

The Chairmen are a nice bunch of lads from The Royal Hospital of Neuro-Disability in Putney. They build, among other things, wheelchairs, hence their team name. Engineers with a conscience – I like it. They are jocular and fun as soon as we talk to them, obviously up for whatever we chuck at them. And we are chucking a real 'curve ball' at these guys.

AND WE ARE CHUCKING A REAL 'CURVE BALL' AT THESE GUYS

That sounds so American it's frightening, but it's very hard for someone as shallow and sponge-like as me not to be influenced by the environment I'm in. I see the new team and say, 'Hi guys, how's it hanging?' and they laugh, but I wasn't trying to be funny. I was trying to be American and it's tragic.

It's all the more tragic because my job on this series is to try to remain English. There is a little anxiety amongst the folks (people back at Channel 4 HQ in London) that the show will look and sound totally American. Oddly, the build area and scrapyard look uncannily like the ones in Canning Town and Brentford. It's already clear to us that unless people are specifically told that this is being recorded in America, they wouldn't even think about it. When we were testing the egg-launchers, we joked off-camera that the San Raphael mountains in the distance were in fact the Malvern hills, shot from an odd angle.

I have taken a little too long to eat my breakfast – I've been standing around gassing with the Chairmen team – and Andrew, our increasingly nervous second assistant director, comes up and delivers a classic American request: 'Robert, totally in your own time, and when you feel absolutely ready, we are approaching the point where, if you were ready, we could go and shoot the opening sequence of today's show. Finish your breakfast first, of course, and when you've really, totally finished, if you could go and get changed and then maybe make your way out to the set, that would be really cool.'

Poor Andrew, he's had a lot of problems adjusting to working with an English crew, where a rather abrupt manner and a fair amount of obscenity have crept into communications over the years. The equivalent request from an English second assistant would be along the lines of: 'Oi, they want you!'

Everyone seems happy, though. The sun is shining. I hurriedly get changed into my costume, which is really comfortable. Cathy is busy with her lipstick, or something, and I don't get involved. She even has a little makeshift make-up table in the wardrobe Portacabin that doubles as our luxury no-expense-spared dressing room. I head quickly for the set, where they are not ready for me. They must have got bored waiting and are now doing something more interesting.

I head back to the coffee machine and meet the still very smart-looking Top Gun team. These fellows all met through their connection with Tornado fighter jets. Two of them, Captain Barry and Scavenger Arthur, still spend their professional lives testing Tornado engines. You don't know what a Tornado is? Well, if you've ever been for a walk in the hills and mountains of Wales or Scotland and a fighter jet has flown five feet above your head and scared the living daylights out of you, that was probably a Tornado.

I can tell the team are going to be fun because when I ask a really dumb question ('What happens when a jet engine won't start? Does it sound like a car that won't start?'), they answer with humour and a lot of information. Apparently, they don't always start. Sometimes they stop working when the jet is in the air, sometimes they even backfire, and when they do they shatter windows and blow out doors in the test building. As Barry is telling me this, a little gaggle of backstage scrappies start to form around him. We all love to hear how

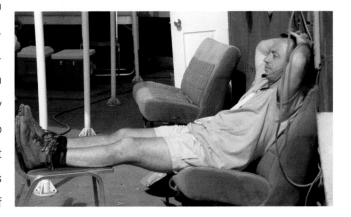

It's non-stop slog on the set.

dangerous 'proper' engineering is, and backfiring Tornado jets have to be at the upper level of extremely loud and impressive things.

'Cool,' says Dom. 'Has anybody ever been blown to bits by a backfire?'

'No, we're very careful,' smiles Barry as though to reassure him, but Dom is disappointed. He has spent a lot of time playing Quake and Counter Strike on the office PC. He loves things like exploding engines and dangerous fighter jets; he once told me he dreams of being a door gunner on a helicopter. I think underneath it all he's a nice boy, but I worry for him.

I have a quick talk with Top Gun scavenger Rob who's the only pilot on the team, although he wasn't a pilot when he was in the RAF. He has trained since he left and now flies cargo all over the world for courier companies.

The Top Guns are very clean-cut, bright-eyed and raring to go. The Chairmen, by lucky contrast, are slightly less clean-cut. Some of them are sitting around smoking, but that's not a bad sign. It's impossible to prejudge a team before they are in the middle of a build and they hit a really sticky problem. It's teams that can adapt to circumstances on their feet that seem to survive. Having said that, every rule I have ever suggested for *Scrap*-triumph has always been proved wrong.

'Teams, it's time to launch into action. Set your sights and take aim. Your target today is to build a…'

The Chairmen playing hangman on their whiteboard.

I say this to the camera crew and an empty scrapyard. The teams are being kept well away, they still have no idea what the challenge is; or at least, that's the theory. There have been breaches in *Scrapheap Challenge* security, but we do make a huge effort to ensure that neither team has a clue what they are going to build before the go moment.

I am announcing the challenge to myself because the opening sequence is recorded about five times to ensure that the director (on this episode the wonderfully calm and encouraging David Mitchell) has enough angles to cut the whole thing together. If there's one thing cameramen hate, it's seeing another cameraman in their shot. This is an endless problem on the show because there are so many cameras and so many camera operators.

The Top Guns prefer noughts and crosses.

So to record the opening, all the cameras start on one side looking at myself and Cathy, then everyone moves around and faces the other way to record the teams' arrival.

It's the most frustrating time for the teams. They turn up at the crack of dawn, get changed into their spotless boiler suits, they're all ready in their team colours and all the other stuff so they can be filmed walking through the yard – which takes all of five minutes. Then they have to wait around for ages while Cathy and I go through the fake start procedure. Even when they finally come out and get told what the challenge is, they can't actually start because they have to run into the yard about three times and pretend to start so we can cover all the angles without a camera operator in the picture.

Finally, it's time to start for real. One more time, Cathy and I explain what they have to do: 'Teams, it's time to launch into action. Set your sights and take aim. Your target today is to build a... totally terrific torpedo.'

Whose idea was this? Build a torpedo in a day – not only an underwater machine that has to achieve neutral buoyancy, but has to have engines that work and a remote control steering system to guide it. It's not necessarily big, but it's hugely complex and there are millions of things that could go wrong. I love it.

The teams run into their work areas and gather around their whiteboards as Cathy and I hide behind the set listening to every word they say. This is a crucial part of the day, because the overall strategy of the teams is decided during this period.

The idea is that the expert's carefully worked-out plan is discussed and hopefully acted upon. But there have been cases where the team have totally rejected the plan, and there are no rules against this. In the previous series there was a classic example, when Bowser and the Filth, a team of London police officers, threw out the design their expert had come up with for a high-powered rugby ball kicker, settling instead for an even higher-powered catapult. The result? Disaster for Bowser and the Filth. The machine failed to work and their rugby ball barely made it off the end of the launcher.

This time it's evident that this won't happen. I listen to the Top Guns team, who are listening carefully to their expert, David Jackson. David works for BAE systems, a weapons manufacturing company. He specializes in making mine detection equipment, but has considerable experience with torpedoes.

As he talks to them I start to lose the plot. They are using a lot of jargon that I'm not familiar with – specialist technical terms. As I concentrate, I can see he is referring to concepts such as: if you put a propeller on one end of a tubey thing and put it in water, it's not going to move forward – the propeller will stay still because it's meeting more resistance in the water, and the tubey thing will just spin around, going nowhere. He is suggesting they use a lump of iron on the torpedo body as a sort of keel, and a floaty thing on the surface to counteract the turning of the tube. The team seem to like this. They have had no previous experience of making anything similar and are happy to go along with him.

Once the team have agreed on their plan, the captain sends the scavengers off to find the bits they need. Again, this moment has to be filmed more than once. As soon as the six-wheeled ATVs roar off into the distance, they have to turn around and come back to do it again. However, after the second time that's it, the clocks start and we stop for nothing.

I HAVE TO PICK MY WAY ACROSS MOUNTAINS OF TRASH

The Top Guns scavengers – diminutive but dogged Arthur Buckton and dashing pilot Robert Baskerville – prove themselves to be some of the best in the business. In minutes the Top Gun build area is littered with electric motors, wire, lumps of plastic

They still look gung ho, and this is take 107!

and steel tubing, propellers, large slabs of polystyrene and weirdly moulded bits of non-absorbent foam. By the time I go in to talk to the captain and expert about their plan, I have to pick my way across mountains of trash.

My job at this time is to act as a channel between someone like expert David and the viewing public, whose grasp of the finer points of torpedo design may be somewhat lacking. I blame the education system – I managed to leave school with very little experience in the field and I've suffered because of it. All my torpedoes have been rubbish.

They take me through the design very clearly, I ask stupid questions and they answer them clearly. Very good. They even stand in the right place for the cameras. Backstage, I check on the state of play with director David, Cathy and producer Jeremy. I learn that there are serious problems with the Chairmen. Clearly, their scavenging skills aren't up to those of the Top Guns. They have one bit of broken plastic tube, a battery that we know doesn't work and no electric motors of any sort.

I glance through one of the little spy windows on the set and they do look rather glum. It's nothing new, in fact it's a classic *Scrap* situation and at this early stage of the contest it means absolutely nothing.

Hmm, polystyrene. Obviously a vital component for a submarine.

I hear a series of clicking, whistling and quacking noises behind me and know without looking that it's none other than Peter Clews, a *Scrapheap* stalwart of many years' standing. For someone who can at first appear to be on day release, Peter has an enormous amount of responsibility for the show as production manager. He's one of those men who never seems to lose their cool, even when just about everything seems to be going wrong. The teams all know him because it's his job to do the safety briefing first thing in the morning. In fact, it seems to be his job to do most things – carry food around, buy toilet paper, clean up empty drink cans and do funny walks every now and then for no obvious reason.

'What's happening, then?' he asks. It's part of the peculiarity of the show that half the people working on it have no idea what is going on the other side of the wooden wall that separates the teams from the rest of the crew.

'One side is building a torpedo, and the other side is busy building a torpedo,' I reply helpfully.

'OK, yes. I get the picture,' says Peter. 'So what's the challenge?'

'They've got to build a rubber aeroplane. Didn't I say?'

'Of course, it's the oil rig challenge,' says Peter. He clicks his fingers twenty-two times in a circle while standing on one leg. His remark is interspersed with a series of Cartoon Channel clangs and honks. I think it's his way of releasing tension. Peter has spent the three months before we all arrive making sure we *can* arrive – getting visas, tickets, work permits; making sure we have somewhere to live when we do by finding several clusters of apartments over the greater Los Angeles basin; making sure the teams can make stuff by supplying all the tools they need; making sure there's something to eat when we need lunch; making sure there are toilets, tea and coffee, electricity and lights when it gets dark, a fire officer and a medic on hand the whole time anyone is on the site… I could go on.

Peter walks away with one hand flapping around uncontrollably, making more honking, hissing and grunting noises. I notice a few members of the American crew staring at him with mid-level alarm. They must think we are all a little odd.

Director David informs me it's time for a judge chat. I have already met the judge, he's an ex-submarine captain called Commander Mike Finney who now works for the Royal Navy's public relations department. He appeared on the news a great deal during the attempts to rescue the doomed crew of the Russian nuclear submarine the *Kursk*. As soon as we talk, I can see why he got the gig. He's a very good talker, he explains things beautifully and, of course, has the advantage of first-hand experience of real torpedoes.

A very cool and charming man... and Robert. Captain Mike Finney surveys the scene.

We go on to the set and settle on the throne, as it's lovingly called. There's a site plan scrawled on the back of the set to help the new camera operators find their way around and, earlier in the day, Peter Clews pointed something out: someone had spelt throne with a 'w', so it said 'thrown'. But no one was prepared to admit to it. The English crew decided it must be an American, the Americans were sure it must be the other way around. I stepped in and tried to reduce the tension by claiming that I did it. Peter explained that they knew it couldn't have been me because I wouldn't have been able to spell the word 'plan', which appears above the drawing.

Judge Mike Finney and I settle on to the 'thrown' and start to discuss the situation. I make a mental note of the seemingly inordinate amount of submariners we've had on the show. Three last week in the Storm Force team, and now Commander Mike. He's really good and can repeat an answer again and again just as freshly as the first time, which is not an easy thing to do. If cameras or sound go wrong, we often have to repeat things. It's easy to ask a question again, but not so easy to repeat the answer as though you're still making it up naturally. He's clearly done this sort of thing before.

Some of the judges we've had are brilliant at what they do, but maybe not so hot at communicating their knowledge. The television camera is a very cruel, very unforgiving machine. Every nuance of what you say is picked up; every flicker of the eyes as you try to remember what to say is recorded in minute detail. The camera takes the viewer much closer to your face than someone listening to you in normal conversation ever would. (Unless you're speaking to series producer Jeremy Cross, who actually does stand very close to you. Maybe he's worked in telly so long that he lines up his eyes like a camera operator lines up a shot. He wants you to fill his screen so he more or less stands on your feet when he talks to you.)

On the throne, judge Mike explains things I never knew about torpedoes. They have contra-rotating screws on the back so that the tube of the torpedo doesn't spin around in the water. He tells me of a Russian-made torpedo that can travel through the water at 400 knots over a short distance. I'll have to tell Dom about that.

Mike is very keen on the Top Guns design, a single electric motor powered by batteries that remain on dry land, connected to the torpedo by a long wire that plays out behind. I always make the judge put money on one team and Mike's is firmly on the Guns. Not surprising really, because by this time there is precious little evidence on the Chairmen's side of anything resembling, well, anything.

Now that looks like a torpedo.

By lunchtime, the mood in the Chairmen's camp is reaching an all-time low. When I go in to speak with them, their expert, Steve Takel, who normally works in the marine division of the DERA (Defence Evaluation Research Agency), is looking at a bit of plastic tubing and scratching his head.

It turns out he was planning to build a torpedo with three electric motors – one main driving one and two smaller ones to act as rudders. So far, they have no motors and only a few bits of wire and a broken model aircraft. The team's scavengers, Gerard and Ron, are out on the heap turning it upside down looking for anything that could be used to power their torpedo.

I don't want to tell Gary Derwent, the team captain, that the Top Guns next door have more electric motors than you can poke a stick at and that they're only using one. But I tell him anyway.

ANDREW'S IN A BIT OF A PANIC, LOOKING AT HIS WATCH

The team's mood improves considerably when the delightful Ron returns with the engine from an electric-powered outboard motor. This is just what they need and the team are suddenly galvanized into action.

I come off the set after talking to the Chairmen and Andrew, the second assistant director, runs up to me. He's really trying hard to keep us up to speed about when we are needed, but occasionally, just because of the odd way we've developed of doing the show, he will miss a beat. Throughout the show I make an announcement every hour, telling the teams how much build time they have remaining, and I've just given the five-hour call. At the start of the day, we tell them the hour has passed every fifty minutes or so, just to get them going. We've seen teams sit around gassing because they still have nine hours left, only to find them in a blind panic when they have one hour left and they've barely started. To cope with this, the hours start to grow a little towards the end of the day and we enter 'Scraptime'.

Andrew's in a bit of a panic, looking at his watch: 'Robert, we really need you to go on and do the five-hour call, like now.'

'Just done it, Andrew,' I say, as kindly as I can. I really don't want to put the guy down and make him feel bad because he is so nice and considerate. He folds up in embarrassment when he hears this and I feel lousy. We've been doing the hourly calls for years and somehow it all happens on the nod of the head, or when director David taps his watch and holds up five fingers.

This year, though, there is a difference to the time call. Just before I announce the call, I pull down a giant lever situated to the side of the throne, which, through a satisfyingly complex system of pulley wheels and steel wire, turns a rusting metal peacock on the other side of the throne. On the peacock's bottom is a countdown clock made up of a foot-shaped plate, which points at the numbers arranged around the iron tail feathers.

Cameraman Mike Todd and I try to work out new and innovative ways to record the time calls, like new camera angles and positions for me to be in. I notice Top Gun captain Barry giving me a look as we go through our antics. At first I imagine it's because he thinks we're a couple of prats and he's wondering why Mike isn't filming the real action. I later discover it's because the Top Guns have reached a bit of a crisis.

'What it is, you see,' says Jeremy when I get outside the set, 'is that the Top Guns can't find enough wire. They need over 180 feet of electric cable to run their torpedo and they can't find any.'

'Is there any on the set?' I ask stupidly.

'Tons. They keep walking past it,' says Jeremy in utter delight. 'It's brilliant.'

This may sound cruel, but it means there's a bit of drama and that's what we all love. When I first started doing the show it used to tie me up in knots, knowing where something the teams vitally needed was hidden. I'd see them looking really worried and I'd be desperate to show them where everything was, just to make them happy. I've hardened. I'm tough now, and I can watch them suffer with only the merest glimmer of empathy. That's what *Scrapheap* has done to me – turned me into an unfeeling swine.

THAT'S WHAT SCRAPHEAP HAS DONE TO ME – TURNED ME INTO AN UNFEELING SWINE.

After lunch, the Top Gun team were soaring away in the lead and the tragic Chairmen were sitting around moaning; but the situation has now completely reversed, as so often happens. The Chairmen are now very busy actually making something. Admittedly it's a slightly unusual plan – a torpedo with a chimney pot that's designed to stick out of the water, with one engine on an arm sticking out of the side to steer with. But they're happy. Meanwhile, the Top Gunners are spending hours untangling bits of trash wiring that their expert David doesn't think is going to be any good, but it's all they've got. Their build seems to have ground to a halt as they all try to work out what to do.

The reason they want the batteries on dry ground beside them and a wire leading to the torpedo is very sensible. Lead acid batteries give off hydrogen gas. If they're in a confined space (like a watertight tube) and there's a spark in the compartment, you have a fairly effective bomb – which wasn't the challenge.

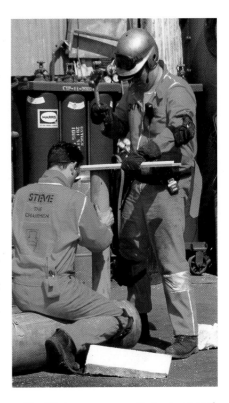

The Chairmen prepare their covert surf board attachment.

The judge gives me this piece of information by the coffee machine in the little shed at the back of the set. Who is standing next to him but Dom, wearing an outlandish covert infiltrators outfit and a T-shirt with the words 'Green Piece' printed on it. Yes, I did spell that correctly. Between the two words is the image of a green hand-gun. 'Green'... 'Piece'. Cool, Dom. I want one.

'A bomb? How dangerous?' asks Dom.

'Oh, it would be very dangerous, but don't worry, we won't let it happen.'

'Shame,' says Dom. 'I think we should have a challenge where they have to build a really powerful bomb. That would be excellent.'

Anyway, the reason the Chairmen have their chimney is to let any hydrogen gas escape from inside the torpedo, whereas the Top Guns don't have batteries inside theirs. Until now. It may be that they will have to radically alter their design over halfway through the build.

Cathy and I sit on the throne for one of our chats. We never talk to each other beforehand or prepare anything, and sometimes we can waffle on a bit. Oh, all right then, we waffle on for so long that some camera operators have collapsed in boredom. Just before we start, camera maestro Mike Todd tells us something he heard about the previous shoot. The new sound mixer, who is not used to the, let's say, idiosyncratic way that Cathy and I do our little chats, turned our microphones down mid-way through our talk. He was so sure we were having a private conversation that he thought it only polite. Of course we had to do the whole thing again,

The Chairmen sitting on an old sewage pipe. Nice.

which was fine because we droned on in a totally new way the second time.

However, this event underlined something important about the show. When you think about it, in some ways it proves that we are doing things right, in that we aren't speaking any differently on camera than at any other time, which is what we are trying to achieve. On the other hand it implies that what we are saying is so banal that he couldn't believe anyone would think it worthy of committing to tape. He may have a point.

As the sun starts to set, the Chairmen have found another electric motor, a tiny little thing that must have come off a toy aeroplane. It has a little propeller on it that doesn't look like it was designed to do much underwater, but it's all they've got and they are happy.

The Top Guns' camp is a mass of twisted wire and what looks like hundreds of slices of baguette bread. This turns out to be bits of foam floaty stuff they are joining to their wire in order to make sure it floats as it's played out behind their torpedo. It's taken Arthur ages to untangle the wire then twist it all together. He walks out into the yard with it to stretch it out and see how much they've got. It looks like loads, but it would be a real pain, as he points out, if they ran out of wire before the torpedo reached its target.

By the time I do my final chat with challenge judge Mike Finney, the build is nearing completion. Very unusually for a judge, he completely changes his mind about which team he has his money on. When they started, he was behind the Top Guns, and it made sense – their build was very methodical and organized. Their torpedo looked good, they had all the ingredients they needed to make a top-class *Scrapheap* machine. However, as the odd-looking multi-engined craft the Chairmen have built starts to take shape, Mike changes his mind. Instead of putting £10 on the Top Guns, he's decided to put £2.50 on the Chairmen.

I call 'time'. The teams are so exhausted they can barely raise a cheer. First assistant director Gerard tries to gee them up for a second stab at this tumultuous moment.

'OK guys, when Robert calls time, let's really hear it, yeah. Wow, yeah, all right!'

I call time again and they sort of half-cheer, half-whimper. You can't blame them – they have been struggling away to build complex machines for ten hours. It's cold, we're all tired, it's a wrap.

The Test

For once, I do not have to get up at the very crack of dawn to get to the test site. My call time is 8.30am, a doddle. I check out the location on my endless map of LA and set off.

Down the 101 for about 60 miles, never leaving the city. It's big, this place. We are recording the torpedo test at an enormous swimming pool and leisure park. One of those places with twisty black tubes that semi-naked individuals hurl themselves down. It's quiet and slightly eerie when we arrive; theme parks always are when they're closed to the public. I never go to them when they're open – I just seem to film in them when they're empty and silent.

This one is still closed for the winter, although that generally sounds a bit crazy in LA as they don't really have a winter like we do. Not a proper one. But as we

Not exactly an action-packed start to the Test day.

Cathy and the Top Guns with the ultimate weapon.

approach the park, a huge dark cloud is looming up towards us. By the time we get out of the car, the first very big, very cold drops of rain are falling.

But stuff the weather; the teams are very sparky, everyone is very sparky. It's amazing what a bit of sleep can do. The teams have had a weekend to themselves – they've been to Disneyland and on the Universal Studios tour and all those sorts of things. I've been up the coast to Santa Barbara to see Bob Collector, a screenwriter friend and his family. As soon as I actually meet people outside the teams and crew, I am amazed by their fascination with the show. Bob has seen all the series and knows all the different challenges we have attempted, and he has plenty of suggestions for teams and challenges.

'You should have an upper-class team and a working-class team. We'd love to see that here, some really posh English toffs having to get their hands dirty actually making something, and some of your normal people who'd be used to like, dirt and hard work, right?'

I know Bob is fascinated by the British class system but I'm not sure it would work. We've talked about doing special one-offs, like a celebrity *Scrapheap*. Say, Stephen Fry as captain of a team with Carolyn Quentin and Lee Evans, versus Jonathan Ross and a team of Ainsley Harriet and Dawn French. It's never happened. It might be easy to say that celebs have seen how hard the teams work and probably don't fancy it, but I know a few who would be very keen to dive in and have a go.

I inspect the pool where the launching is going to take place. There's no sign of the battleships yet, but I don't worry about it. The idea is that each team will stand on a collapsible platform at either end of the pool. In front of them will be a model battleship that will explode in a shower of water and 'sink' if the opposing team's torpedo hits it three times in a row.

During normal Californian weather, neither team would mind this prospect; in fact, if they had any sense they'd dive in anyway. But we are not experiencing normal Californian weather, we are experiencing normal Yorkshire weather, and North Yorkshire at that. It's teeth-chatteringly cold in the pool and I am glad that there are no plans for me to get in it. Cathy, however, is not so lucky. She has somehow landed the job of swimming around the pool during the test to make sure there's no foul play.

After I've changed and been fitted with all the sound equipment, I see that there has been some progress on the battleship front, but not much. The framework that the ships are mounted on was supposed to have been delivered at 6.00am, but it didn't arrive until after 10.00am. The story is heart-breaking and somehow classic of anything connected to *Scrappers*. The special effects man, Roger Matsuo, had a crisis the week before when his huge truck, which contains all his tools, broke down after he'd finished a shoot in Arizona. The tow truck that came to rescue him broke its tow hook and he was stranded, so he flew back to LA and built the rig we are using with borrowed tools on borrowed time. He looks a bit bleary, and that's because he hasn't slept for two days and two nights in order to get the thing ready.

Clint McLean, the long-standing *Scrapheap Challenge* art director, is already in his wetsuit in the water, sorting everything out. Clint has been on the show for two years and has proved

Arthur from the Top Guns faces up to the possibility of imminent dampness.

himself to be the most diligent, committed and good-natured of art directors. All the trophies that we give out at the end of each series – many of which are part of the set and anything made of metal (the new timer peacock for example) are made by Clint. He is a tall, broad-shouldered South African, crowned with a great mop of tied-back blonde dreadlocks. Always easy to pick out in a crowd, is Clint. He and designer Annabel Mazzotti are related through marriage: Clint's wife is Annabel's sister. It's all very incestuous once you realize what's going on. None of my wives, sisters, children, aunties or anyone else works on *Scrapheap*, but a lot of the crew have roped in members of their family to do odd jobs. I pretend I don't mind, but underneath it all I'm bitter, obviously.

Annabel and Clint have been living up in the mountains outside LA while building the set. Probably in some isolated adobe hut with a grass roof – they wouldn't dream of staying in an apartment with running water and a heated pool. They are all kind of nomad, hippy set-builders, if such a thing can exist. Annabel normally lives in Melbourne, Australia, where she's involved in building a sort of giant, modern Stonehenge in the middle of the bush. Clint lives in England, but also in Africa – Mozambique, to be precise – where he has helped build a school and set up some sort of amazingly beneficial education institute for the local people. He is one of those people I have always wanted (but failed) to be like – a really good person who actually does stuff to help people who are less fortunate, without making a song and dance about it.

Today he is helping people who are probably more fortunate than a lot of us, but who have screwed up. The steel framework for the battleship targets is finally being manhandled painstakingly into the water. It's one of those weird pools that has a wave machine at one end, and a sort of sloping concrete 'beach' at the other. Clint is there, standing in the pouring rain in his wetsuit, trying to get it into position. I have never seen him looking more miserable – no matter how tired he is, no matter how long he's been working, he's always smiling and ready to joke around. But not today.

And the weather isn't helping. It's tipping it down as the Chairmen test launch 'Gums', as their delightfully daft torpedo has been named. I assume it's called Gums because although they have painted big fangs on the nose cone to make it look like a shark, they know it's pretty harmless. Also, team member Ron used to be a dental technician in New York, so he knows a thing or two about gums and stuff.

As I talk to the teams, rain pouring on my head, my swishy little digital camera is in my pocket getting very wet. I don't just mean splashed on a bit, it ends up half-submerged in a pocket puddle. I don't know a lot about electronics, but it just looks wrong when you lift up your camera and water is pouring out of it.

We have lunch. Very little has happened. This could only take place on a television shoot. In any other industry, if 90 per cent of the workforce stood around gassing for four hours, the whole business would crumble overnight. But that's more or less what's expected in this exasperating business; something has gone wrong, so the best way to handle it is to stand around telling stories about extreme experiences. Mike Finney manages to top the lot of us. He reveals how easy it is to spot a group of submariners relaxing in a large empty hotel bar. However much space there is in the room, they will always be squashed together in a corner. That's what they're used to and they don't feel safe if they spread out too much. He's also taken all those SAS boys around the world, especially during the Falklands War – arriving on the coast in the middle of the night and letting them zoom off in their little rubber boats, festooned with guns and missile launchers. Very Bravo Two Zero. Of course, Dom picks up on this and moves closer; he doesn't want to miss any juicy tit-bits about war and guns.

Boom... There goes the midships!

During lunch I talk to Dom's girlfriend, Marie-Louise Frellesen, a very bright Danish woman. Someone is smoking near us and she explains how she gave up thirteen years ago, and how Dom has never smoked. I'm surprised, because Dom seems to have a death wish, but apparently he's fervently anti-smoking.

'He doesn't smoke,' she says with a gentle smile, then adds, as if suddenly remembering, 'Of course, he's completely mad, but he doesn't smoke.'

Eventually the rain actually stops, but it's still pretty parky and no one is that excited. It does dampen your spirits if you sit around in the rain for long enough, and we've all been hanging around for ages. All of us except Clint, who is now neck-deep in water. His skin has actually turned blue as he struggles away with the special effects team to make the battleship targets look at least half-decent.

I make my way to one of the platforms to do my opening piece. There must be fifty people watching – the teams, the crew, the people who own the water park. I can't blame them; there's not much else going on. After all my talk about the awful way TV presenters speak, I come out with the most presenter-ish three lines I have ever delivered. I put on that silly presenter voice, I breathe in all the wrong... huh... places. I think it's dire. I catch Cathy's eye and I can see I am not wrong.

'I think I'll do that again,' I say.

'I think that might not be a bad idea,' says Cathy. David the director is obviously relieved. He wasn't happy with it either, but as each director only does one, or at most two shows per series, they are often a little less sure of telling Cathy and I what to do. They already have such a huge workload keeping track of the two teams, the huge camera crew, the sound department and all the engineering problems, and the last thing they want to think about it is the people who talk into the camera lenses every now and then.

It is, essentially, embarrassing to look into a camera lens as opposed to a human face and speak as though you're talking directly to one individual. I think that's basically what you have to do, although it's hard to tell. Speaking to one individual when potentially millions are watching is a fairly new psychological experience, so there aren't really any precedents. It's not like being on stage or doing after-dinner talks, it's much more intimate and it really shows if you get it just a bit wrong. A stage is very forgiving; you can get away with more mistakes. A camera is right in there.

Finally, and way later than was planned, both teams get their designs in the water and try them out. The Chairmen are looking very confident. Gums achieves the semi-impossible by being almost perfectly neutrally buoyant. They have to add a couple of weights to trim it up, but it's very close. As soon as they switch on the remote control it's clear they have a serious contender. Gums just flies through the water, they have a great deal of control, forwards, backwards, left and right. Although it's the bigger engine on one arm that ends up doing the steering, the little one is very cute. It's like a baby turtle, just learning to use its little flippers, splashing about in the water every now and then to no apparent effect.

The team are very confident but very cold. I trot through the rain to the other side of the large pool we are using to see the Top Gun torpedo slip into the water. Again they have made a very serviceable craft; it rests beautifully under the surface, only its 'stealth' surfboard showing above the water. The engine kicks into life and the torpedo moves forward, but not, apparently, in any other direction. The rudders don't seem to be having an enormous effect, positioned as they are to either side of the propeller.

Add to that the drag of the electric cable and the floats that run out from behind the torpedo, and the Top Guns are in serious trouble.

'We need a bigger rudder,' says expert David Jackson.

We always allow the teams a little 'tinker time', as we refer to it, once their machines are *in situ*. Tinker time is sometimes a

Two deadly vessels gliding by each other rather gracefully.

Did the best men win?

minute or two as they paint part of the machine, or make sure essential bolts are tight and fuel tanks are full. On other occasions, tinker time can be quite long, like when some part of the machine has manifestly failed to work: say, the rudder of a torpedo. Clearly, the Top Guns don't have a chance unless they can steer at least a bit, and if they don't have a chance we don't have a competition.

While they create a makeshift rudder in a matter of minutes (weird how this never seems to happen on a build day), Clint and the special effects men are still struggling away in the pool. Clint now looks really unhappy. He is in a wetsuit, which, in theory, keeps you warm in the water. In practice, if you are in cold water and it's raining even colder water and you've been in it for hours, things start to go really wrong. Roy Irwin, our medic, puts a weird electronic gizmo in Clint's ear when he finally emerges. He is worried. Clint's core body temperature is down to just 90° Fahrenheit. That's clearly not a good thing and Clint is sent off to have a warm shower.

But he's done it, the battleships are in position, the teams take up their positions – Top Guns complete with new and amazingly effective rudder. Cathy is in the water and looking very happy about it; she is also in a wetsuit and is being very stoical about the cold.

Andrew, our ever-ready second assistant director, asks myself and judge Mike if we would like to 'sashay over to the judge's area'. This makes Mike laugh very richly; I doubt it's the sort of suggestion that's made to a naval officer on a regular basis.

I explain the rules of the game to the teams while standing on one side of the pool with Mike. The crew and cameras are on the other side looking across. I sound the very sophisticated *Scrapheap Challenge* air horn – which is actually me making a horrible honking noise through a loud hailer – and the Top Guns, who we have elected to go first, release their weapon.

'It's not what you'd call fast,' says Mike Finney, as we stand in silence and watch in fascination. He's right. The torpedo approaches the enemy battleship very slowly and steadily. It reaches it eventually, actually managing to pull the great long strip of floats that are attached to its power cable.

The battleship model does nothing at first, but then suddenly there is a burst of water and the section hit by the torpedo falls over. Special effects indeed. It is an irony that doesn't miss many of the crew that the machines botched together out of rubbish are working rather well, while the special effects – which cost a great deal of money and were late and don't really work anyway – are rather unsatisfactory.

Now the Chairmen let go of their torpedo and, by comparison, it rockets across the pool. In reality, a good swimmer could overtake it, but I'm impressed. It gently nudges into the enemy ship and, after a brief special effects pause, a fountain of water blasts up behind the section and the score is evened out.

The second round has the same result. This time both torpedoes move in a smoother ark as their pilots get the hang of how to steer them. The Chairmen have an easier task in that they are using a fairly standard radio control handset. The Top Guns are using a board with a lot of wires joined to screws. They touch one wire to another to complete a circuit and the torpedo goes forward; if they touch it to another, the torpedo turns right. It must be very difficult but they manage to do it.

This means that the third round is a death-match shoot-out. Both teams have to release their torpedoes at the same moment and the first one to finally sink the enemy battleship is the winner.

The torpedoes leave their pens – well, they leave the hands of Gary of the Chairmen and Arthur of the Top Guns. Both weapons speed towards their target, it's neck and neck. Which team will go on to the next round?

Kabooom!

STREET SWEEPER

On a five-minute break during the build day for the egg shooter challenge, I joined a group of friendly-looking people who were sitting around a makeshift table. Jeremy Cross, series producer; Helen Williamson, Jason Gibb and Nat Grouille, assistant producers and fast-rising stars in the *Scrapheap* heavens; production supervisor and madman Peter Clews; and Tom Hogan, the badly bruised location manager. They were discussing rubbish and how to distribute it: 'Obviously, we need cans, bottles and paper, but I think large pieces of masonry could be a problem.'

'We can get cans easy enough, but do we need to have the rubbish sorted into sub-genres?'

'I think it's basically mix and match.'

'I know a guy who can supply us with 40 tons of pre-washed cans, or 30 tons of pre-washed plastic bottles.'

'Pre-washed. Marvellous.'

'40 tons! Isn't that too much?'

'It's like a truckload.'

'What about gravel?'

'Gravel is good! Yes, gravel, we've got to have gravel.'

'Gravel is easy. Bark chippings?'

'Oh, I'd say bark chippings are a must-have. And Clint says he'll bring his compost bin with him so we can have some really manky vegetable peelings.'

**'PRE-WASHED.
MARVELLOUS.'**

In any other circumstances, overhearing a conversation like this might make you discreetly move to another table, but this is *Scrappers* and you have to take it in your stride. What the production team were actually discussing was the test for this week's challenge. It's a great example of the level of preparation that takes place before the teams arrive.

When I arrive on set on the build day it's still dark, but I'm really looking forward to this challenge. The Chaos Crew have arrived and are already in their overalls. It's very hard to always be utterly fair and not have favourite teams on the show, and I try my best to be impartial. However, every now and then, teams or team members have such extreme skill or sharp humour that they naturally stick in your mind. Andy, John and Spike of the Chaos Crew fall into that category they're very unassuming Yorkshiremen who make

Aye up. Stand back, it's the Chaos Crew.

no effort to be funny or clever, but who are both. As soon as I see them and shake hands, it's enormously refreshing to hear their Yorkshire accents this far away from Doncaster. They don't seem particularly nervous or excited, and I'm immediately reminded that I am a *bona fide* poncified Southerner as I twitter on.

I later discuss the Chaos Crew's popularity with Jeremy. We have both discovered that a lot of women admit to fancying the team and we decide it's because they don't say much. Jeremy and I are so in touch with our feminine side that we spout off at any opportunity like two old dears at a bring-and-buy sale, which, we theorize, is NOT what women want. They may say they want men who share their feelings and are sensitive and aware, but what they actually want is someone like Spike. He doesn't really say anything but he does a great deal.

For instance, if you were a woman and I gave you a bunch of flowers, I'd tell you how I was worried about the colour, how I'd tried to get a vase for them but couldn't find the one I wanted; I'd waffle on about how they smell nice but that the scent might be a bit overpowering and if it's a problem I'll take them back...

If Spike gave you a bunch of flowers, he'd just hand them to you and say, 'There y'go lass.'

It would say more than fifteen romantic novels.

The team up against these hunks of masculine perfection are the Catalysts, three engineers from Jaguar. We heard a report from Jackie Morris, who met them at the airport, that instead of piling into the back of the old Honda Civic like the other teams, they were met by representatives of Jaguar USA who supplied them with a twinkling Jaguar S series saloon car each. Not one between them, so they'd argue about who would drive, but one each. It was one of those pieces of information that can leave petrol-heads like most of us on *Scrapheap* sitting in momentary silence.

On Sunday night we all have a meal cooked by Nat, Jackie's boyfriend. It's a hardcore *Scrapheap* gathering and we are talking about farting, obviously. Jackie turns up late; she's just back from meeting the new teams off the plane from England at the airport. She tells us:

'The blokes from the Jaguar team were given a big Jaguar each!'

'Each!' we all shout.

'What type? What type of Jag?'

'An S type.'

'They had one each?! Like, to drive themselves?!' says Spud, spluttering on his corn chips.

'Yeah. One each.'

Long silence…

We never really got over it. I felt a bit intimidated about meeting them, thinking they might be really posh and expect executive treatment, they might be used to being called 'Sir' and having things done for them. If this turned out to be the case, they'd

Up and at 'em – the very keen Catalysts.

be in for a rude shock on this show and I felt awkward.

When I actually meet Garry, Tim and Shane it's an instant relief. They are engineers, they are very funny, irreverent, cheeky with each other and very soon with me and Cathy too. I feel very relaxed with them and everything is looking good.

Almost before I am fully awake I am standing on the set with Cathy. Mike Todd, the camera operator who covers the two of us most of the time, has set up a dolly and track, the sort of mini-railway line that a camera travels along to get a moving, smooth, interesting shot. Even if there's only me in it. We are about to introduce the challenge when I remember something important. I tell this week's director, Matt, that last week the Top Guns overheard my dulcet tones when I was introducing the torpedo challenge, which is precisely not what is supposed to happen. The idea is that when the teams first hear the challenge, they're being recorded, so we can capture that moment of realization when they hear what they've got to do.

Runners are immediately sent scrabbling about looking for team members to make sure they are out of earshot. We do the intro, the teams are brought in and we tell them what they've got to build.

'You have to build a monster cleaning machine, a street sweeper!'

The Chaos Crew look thrilled – a big dirty machine made of metal with big engines and a lot of noise, oil and dirt, possibly some flames and a small explosion thrown in for effect.

Gratifyingly, the Catalysts also look very pleased with the notion. Used as they are to building very sleek, very fast cars with a lot of state-of-the-art gadgetry under the hood, it might be fair to assume a humble street sweeper is below them, but they're totally up for it.

Cathy bangs the 'dong', as it's rather awkwardly been named, and the teams run into their build areas. For the next ten minutes the two of us listen carefully to what the teams say. We need to know what they plan to do, and this is when each team's expert is in the limelight. I listen to the Chaos Crew while Cathy tunes into Catalyst FM. The Chaos expert, Mike Hasler, is chief engineer in a company that manufactures street cleaners, so he knows his rubbish. He suggests a kind of mechanical dustpan and brush that they can just drive along, collecting tons of rubbish as they go. It's a tubular brush that sweeps along the street, set near a kind of reverse elevator with paddles instead of steps. These paddles carry the rubbish up and into a collection bin. The Chaos Crew ask some good questions, but they're clearly sold on the idea.

It's all very straightforward, and after the usual shenanigans with false starts, the teams roar off out into the yard on their ATVs. There's nearly an accident right away as both teams reach a narrow gap between two huge piles of scrap. Spike is driving one ATV, Tim from the Catalysts is driving the other Spike gives way and the Catalysts roar off around the corner (for no obvious reason, it has to be said). Spike quietly ties a Land Rover to the ATV and drags it back into the Chaos build area.

Within, I am pretty sure, seven minutes of the start of the competition, the floor of the Chaos build area is flooded with petrol. Andy has been topping up the petrol tank to try out the engine, not spotting the huge hole in the bottom of it. Fire officers in asbestos suits are running around with foam guns, Spike is about to light a welding torch and people are screaming. We know the Chaos Crew are back.

During their last visit to the heap, they destroyed the set. They flooded everywhere they went with gallons of hydraulic fluid, engine oil, petrol and diesel. They set fire to the entire work area when Spike was cutting through thick sheets of steel with an oxy torch – a white-hot lump of metal fell on the sturdy rubber pipes that carry the gas to the gun. They blasted holes in the steel floor by accident, and threw massive lumps of steel about like confetti. The camera crew were scared to go anywhere near them.

As I watch them this time, I can see it's not because they're clumsy or stupid, they are just incredibly focused. They have a task to do and they do it; anything peripheral to that may get torched, trodden on, drilled, mangled and discarded. When I go in to see the team, I talk to team captain Andy and Mike Hasler. They explain the rudiments of the design to me. It's a kind of reverse, brush-activated combine trash harvester. A framework will be built on to the

A Landy! We'll be havin' that reet now...

back of the Land Rover, which will hold a conveyor belt, which will lift the rubbish up and into a container. A circular brush will spizzle around to help flick the rubbish into the conveyor's grip. I am just beginning to understand the idea when I feel something hot on my leg. I look down to see Spike with his trusty oxy torch cutting off the back end of the Land Rover. I just happen to be in the path of a trail of sparks; no way did he do it on purpose, he just didn't know I was there.

... so as we can cut it to bits.

'You carry on, Spike,' I quip as I move back a little.

'Will do,' says Spike without faltering.

'Best keep clear,' says Andy kindly. 'You know Spike, if there's welding to be done, nowt'll stop him.'

I check the board and Andy shows me the special equation that Spike has worked out to help them on the challenge. Clearly, after seeing teams like the Nerds in the previous series, the Chaos Crew felt their approach might not be scientific enough. So they have put in a bit of effort and have come up with this

"BRING IT THROUGH 'ERE AND GET ON WI' IT,'

classic higher maths notion: 'X times Y equals crude'. As I am chuckling about this, Tim, one of the scavengers for the Catalysts, is getting in a terrible mess right outside the Chaos Crew's build area. He has sort of jammed the six-wheel drive, go-anywhere, do-anything fun buggy into a corner and he can't get it out.

'Bring it through 'ere and get on wi' it,' says John, captain Andy's big brother. So, for the first time in *Scrapheap* history, a member of an opposing team rides their scavenger vehicle through the enemy's build area. Tim is pulling a trailer with a large bore hose and some sort of fitting attached that's come off a giant Hoover, which Andy and John promptly steal. Tim doesn't seem to notice at first, and as he crashes back out into the yard, I hope that driving isn't in the upper drawers of his skill set. If he builds with the same panache, the Catalysts are in big trouble. Andy hands back the stuff from Tim's trailer in a very gentlemanly way, and Tim departs in a wibbly-wobbly, vaguely homeward direction.

Over in the Catalysts' camp, the team are also moving at breakneck speed in terms of scavenging, but before I can go and talk to them I can see there is a bit of a crisis brewing. Not with the teams, but with the 'management'.

Off-camera and off the set, I can see director Matt, Jeremy Cross and Jason Gibb talking to team captain Garry Preece and Martin Bremner, the Catalysts' expert. They are standing around a kind of fan thing and I know there's trouble. Pretty soon I learn the whole story and it beautifully illustrates an area of contention in the show.

Everyone involved in the show, either behind the scenes or on the screen, teams or production staff, has been asked at some time by members of the viewing public about how much stuff we 'plant' out in the scrapyard. The truth is, as I have said, that we only plant what we know the teams must have in order to complete the challenge. If there is any way they can actually construct the machine out of scrap in the time allowed, then that's what they must do. They only get special technical bits for reasons of safety or simply because it's actually impossible, even for the most brilliant engineers, to make, say, a steam engine in ten hours.

Before this mini-crisis, the Catalysts' expert Martin has suggested that the team make a giant vacuum cleaner that sucks the rubbish off the street. They have found an old Transit van that runs, a little engine to bolt on the back to power their fan, and they have found a fan.

I KNOW THERE'S TROUBLE

There's the rub, because the whole idea of the challenge was to get them to build the impeller fan. Now they've found one, and no one knew it was there. For the first time in the history of the show, instead of a team not finding a planted item that they need to have, they've found a non-planted one that we really don't want them to have. Hence the argy-bargy.

Jeremy is very good at explaining the problem, though, and with down-tilting heads, the two members of the Catalyst team release their golden find. It does seem unfair in some ways; after all, they did legitimately find an ideal bit of kit on the heap, which would have helped them no end.

I look out at the scrapheap and realize how hard it is to know what's out there. Suddenly, it all looks a bit forbidding. Clint has told me that early this morning he found two black widow spiders near our throne area. I still haven't seen one but, clearly, they are around. Cathy and I have developed the habit of kicking things before we touch them. But the discovery of the unplanted impeller blade has brought home how much of a genuine junkyard this place actually is.

After nine hours work, it looks like this.

Shane, the apparently accident-prone member of the Catalysts, sets to work on building an impeller blade from scratch. Not an easy thing to do, because it has to spin at 3,000 revs per minute – quite fast, and if it isn't balanced properly it could tear the engine and the whole machine they are building to pieces. Shane is their head welder and from what Garry says, it sounds like he's very good at it; though, as they say in America, he clearly has a couple of personal safety issues to deal with. Just the week before coming on the show, he tried to listen to an arc-welding gun to see if it was on by holding it up next to his ear. Of course, it was on, and it set fire to his hair. It can't have been that bad, though, because he still has a mop of mad professor hair on his head.

Off the set, all is going well, except that everyone is moaning about the weather, which is still cold and wet. Still, it would be colder and wetter if we were in Canning Town. It's not that bad.

After last week's test day and all the difficulties we had, I have become very interested in how systems fail, and how, very often, this is not the fault of one individual, but the result of a series of minor errors that coagulate until they form a major crisis. I realize that various management gurus have made a mint giving easy tips on how to avoid system failure, clearly to no avail; because all we see around us all the time are small, medium and large system failures. The *Scrapheap* teams are a wonderful test-bed for these sorts of things, as we can guarantee that something will fail; and how you go about fixing it or redesigning it so it hopefully won't fail again is really a human thing, not a mechanical one.

On the monitors in the production office, there are images of the four main cameras on one screen, so we can see more or less everything that's going on. I watch the teams as I sip a styrofoam cup of American coffee and wonder what they can do to minimize failures. It's really hard for them to plan ahead. If you are making something on a production line – a computer, say, or a car or a fridge – you know all the components and where they should go and how long it takes to put them together. On *Scrapheap*, they are literally making it up as they go along; the only plan is a hastily drawn sketch on a whiteboard.

We've already failed in planning for this particular challenge. We've tried to make sure we have a suitable test area, make sure we have the right kind of rubbish, make sure the teams make what we want them to make. But no one knew that under the half-tipped-over lorry, behind a pile of old tyres, under a broken armchair, behind the mass of tangled cables lay a perfect impeller blade that was just what the Catalysts wanted. How could anyone ever foresee that happening? You just have to cope when it does.

There are more and more people coming down to the site to watch the recording of the show, including Tony Martinez, the owner of the scrapyard. A lot of people claim to have seen the series, but it's very hard to judge whether they actually have. It's almost the done thing in Hollywood to say you've seen everything: 'Sure, I've seen your show, I like it, yeah, it's cool.'

There is no known limit to the number of engines the Chaos Crew can get through.

Doesn't really tell you much about their opinions or, in fact, if they've ever set eyes on it. However, TLC, the American broadcaster, are certainly not backward in coming forward when it comes to promoting the show – or at least their version of it, *Junkyard Wars*, presented by Cathy and an American fellow (as opposed to *Schrotzplatz Krieg*, the German version; or the Dutch version, or the Australian version that we think should be called 'Dagheap Challenge'). Before I got to LA, Cathy shot what's called a promo a short film to be shown on TLC to advertise *Junkyard Wars*. TLC spent over a million dollars on it. A huge set with other actors playing frogs or gnomes or something, shot on 35mm film like a real movie. A million dollars. That's more than they spend on the entire series, which seems utterly crazy; but Americans love marketing, and the public seem to appreciate it. The logic goes that if a company is really prepared to spend big-time on getting your attention, then the product must be worth having.

There was a *Junkyard Wars* poster on Sunset Boulevard earlier in the year, high above the buildings – huge, the size of a house. The title was in massive, tall-as-a-tree letters, with life-size 3-D figures of men climbing up piles of rubbish in the background. Underneath was the catchy sting:

'FINALLY, THERE'S GOOD TRASH ON TV.'

Yes, I like it.

It wouldn't work in England, though, at least I hope not. People would think, 'Oh, if they're pushing it this hard it must be rubbish,' or, 'Just to annoy them I won't watch it even though I wanted to in the first place.' That's what I'm like, anyway.

Back on the show, the scavenge and build leading up to lunch are text-book stuff, very fast the teams are working well and everything's going according to plan.

By mid-afternoon, as always, the teams hit some sort of wall of no progress. They are looking busy, there's lots of noise, there are a few more small fires on the Chaos side, but nothing is actually changing. It's the part of the day when we just let them get on and do it. Production meetings take place under the awning to organize the next challenge, or the one after that, which is proving to be a logistical

The Catalysts take a transit van...

... cut and fold...

nightmare. I look into the build area every now and then. There's still nothing you could call a machine; just piles of bits, neatly ordered on the Catalysts' side, cataclysmically messy on the Chaos side.

I discuss the issues with this week's judge, Roger Hoadley, who is also a street sweeping machine manufacturer. We look at the teams, and he explains the essential differences between brushing and sucking, which, to be honest, are not too hard to grasp.

By nightfall, panic is really setting in. There are lots of earnest discussions behind the scenes: 'They'll never finish. I reckon there's another eighteen hours build on that.'

'The Chaos blokes look like they've hardly started.'

'They have a lot of issues with their impeller blades.'

'We'll be here all – beep – night.'

There are discreet chats off-camera between Jeremy and the teams.

'What d'you think guys, 'cos we really need to wrap it up pretty soon?'

The response on the Catalyst side is reasoned: 'As soon as we've mounted our fan, we just have to fix the tubing and we're done.'

Jeremy then goes around to the Chaos side, and almost breaks his leg tripping over a discarded girder that's lying in a bath of axle grease: 'How's it going?'

'We've got a lot on,' says Andy, his smile lighting up a distinctly oily face.

'D'you think you'll finish in time?'

'No chance.'

'Oh God, what are we going to do? Disaster looms.'

'I'd better crack on then.'

'Right, right. OK, panic stations everybody,' says Jeremy to the four team members, who are all so totally focused on their individual tasks they are totally unaware of Jeremy, the cameras, me, Cathy,

... and turn it into a customised rubbish holder. Very slick.

the Los Angeles sunset, or the thousands of birds circling overhead who are heading home after feeding on the massive landfill site we are working near. They can only see one thing the street sweeping machine, which, as so often happens, suddenly starts to take shape.

The Catalysts mount their engine and fan after what seems like hours of inactivity. Suddenly, there's a flurry of activity and they weld on their outrigger seat, fit their suction hose and start up the engine.

Cathy and I deliver a dustbin full of paper, old cans and, oddly, a pair of braces. As the fan spins up and the suction starts, captain Garry holds up the enormous hose and we start throwing rubbish in. The noise is incredible as the fan literally dices cans and shreds paper. Then, when expert Martin throws in the braces, a whole new range of noises emerges. He stops the engine because the buckle attachment on the braces has ripped a hole in the steel sheet that makes up their outlet pipe. It looks like a bullet has hit it.

Clearly there are some safety questions here. They have a fan spinning around at 3000rpm housed inside a steel case. The spinning blade sucks in an enormous amount of air and it also sucks in anything else that can fit into the pipe. It's just that when those things hit the fan, they fly off in all directions at great speed.

'We'll have to weld on a reinforcing plate,' says Garry, turning to an exhausted-looking Shane. Shane has been doing very careful welding all day, making the blade, but they still have thirty minutes left…

'I COULD DO ANOTHER TEN HOURS, GET IT REALLY SPICK AND SPAN'

With five minutes to go, Cathy and I sit on the throne. The activity is now feverish and both teams look dishevelled, but both machines are growing before our eyes. When I call time, the teams don't have the energy to cheer, although they look happy. Stand-in assistant director Rey tries to cajole them into a cheer, 'Just for the cameras.'

They manage as best they can, and that's it. It's a wrap. We did enter *Scrapheap* time towards the end and we have gone slightly over the allotted ten hours, but only by fifteen minutes or so, and what the teams have done is nothing short of miraculous.

The scene is chaotic as the crew start charging around clearing everything up. Cameras are packed away, tapes have to be numbered and moved to a safe location, there is an enormous amount of organizing to do, and more or less everyone has been on the site since 5.30am.

Andy from the Chaos Crew wants to go back in and finish tightening some bolts. 'I could do another ten hours, get it really spick and span,' he says, and I think he's telling the truth.

The Test

On the way to the test site for the street sweeper challenge, Cathy is driving along looking at pick-up trucks. She's going to be living in LA for over a year, and as Los Angelinos spend something like 27 per cent of their waking life in cars, she needs to make sure she has the car that's right for her. She's already had a go in an Audi TT, but felt it was too small and the wrong colour. As we crawl through heavy traffic heading for the freeway, we see a sporty Dodge pick-up with a 5.5 litre V8 engine, and she likes it. It's a dirty brown colour and only one brake light is working, but what has really caught her eye is the 'For Sale' sign stuck in its tinted rear window. Unusually for America, we can't see how much it is or who to contact, because the glass is hard to see through. Normally, if there's one thing Americans really excel in, it's selling stuff.

We follow it down Santa Monica Boulevard, Cathy swerving and overtaking people in a crazy car-chase bid to catch up with the

The Chaos Crew and the mighty Kirb Krawler.

elusive vehicle, but we lose it somewhere near La Cienega. This lust for cars may sound extravagant, but the whole wheels issue is much less costly in America. For a start, petrol only costs about a quarter of what we pay in Britain, and you can lease cars and do all sorts of deals in LA for next to nothing. They have so many of them already, you may as well have one. It's sent Cathy into a tail-spin, as she is a very environmentally aware person and only ever rides a bike in London; but this is LA, the city of the car.

When you have cars, you have to park them somewhere; and when we arrive at the test site we see that this can have quite an impact on the environment, too. There are really big car parks, and there are really, really big car parks next to huge open-air churches in Orange County, Los Angeles. Here, you can stand at one end of a car park and you can't see the other end because of the curvature of the earth. In one small corner, the crew have spread an impressive amount of rubbish. Soft drinks cans, vegetable peelings, gravel, dust, newspapers and magazines, plastic bottles, old shoes and discarded clothing. We have trashed the otherwise pristine environment of this exclusive neighbourhood. From what I can gather from the American members of the crew, Orange County was mainly a fruit farming area until the early eighties, when Ron Reagan managed to secure government funding to develop the Southern Californian region. It's now a very wealthy, very secure area with enormous housing estates surrounded by very high walls, which are only accessible through security gates. Gated communities where all the houses, cars and people who live there are identical.

The Catalysts' cutting edge, and very noisy, street vacuum cleaner.

'It makes me kind of shiver,' says Eve, the American camera assistant. However, some of the cultural discomfort caused by this exclusively middle-class environment is lost on me, because it's nice and warm and there are lots of trees around.

As we start introducing the test of the street sweeping machines to camera, we have to stop because of the number of cars roaring into the car park. They are in the back of shot and not making a noise, but Mike the cameraman thinks we should wait until they've passed. We wait a long time, because not one or two cars enter the car park, but hundreds, then thousands. As my calendar is totally dominated by shooting days and their logistics, I am utterly unaware that it is Good Friday and that therefore some serious church-going is taking place in Orange County. I say church, but it's more like an open-air arena where Aerosmith might be about to do a gig. Carved into the hill opposite us is a massive auditorium where we can now hear a Christian heavy metal band tuning up.

We learn from a very friendly, very smart Orange County Police Officer that the service takes about an hour, which is a relief, as the noise of the singing and music is too great for the sound department. What seems to happen is that people queue up for an hour to get into the car park, then sit for an hour through the service, then queue for another hour to get out. The sight of a British film crew throwing 'trash' all over the place on Good Friday while two groups of burly looking mechanics tinker with odd-looking bodged machines possibly sends a shudder of disquiet through them.

The air has been still all morning until about 11.30am, when a gentle breeze blows up. Nothing terrible; in fact quite pleasant, as the heat from the sun is growing stronger. However, just as all the cars are leaving the massive car park, the wind catches bits of paper and starts to throw them around like a bored kid. Within a couple of minutes we have lost about half the rubbish to the wind – the rubbish that Clint and the engineering team had so laboriously laid out on the ground. Dom gets a hose to wet it down and try to keep it on the ground, but he is fighting a losing battle. Pretty soon, all the trees and cars within a wide, downwind range are decorated with torn sheets of newspaper. It's not pretty. And this is not cheap rubbish – it's special trash from a company in Hollywood that supplies the film industry. This is pre-washed trash, the only sort we are allowed to use, and it costs $10 a sack. Just think, all those times you saw Starsky and Hutch or Cagney and Lacey drive down a litter-strewn alley, they were driving through quality pre-washed trash. Excellent.

While the crew run around grabbing any sheet of blowing newspaper they can, the teams tinker with their machines until lunch. They are both happy with their creations, and choosing a winner at this stage is impossible.

After lunch, judge Roger Hoadley joins me up a high scaffolding tower where we have an excellent view of the competition. Everything is working, the teams are ready and we get a signal from Ron, our Vietnam vet stand-in assistant director: 'OK, Robert, we are up and running, it's all yours, man. Over to you brother.' After a gulp at the

responsibility I have been given, I start the challenge. Suddenly the Catalysts are waving their hands around in a panic. The challenge is halted and it takes me a couple of seconds to find out why.

'The Catalysts' engine won't start,' Cathy tells me over the walkie-talkie. This was the engine of a Transit van, which had, from the moment they scavenged it off

Panic breaks out as a trash cyclone blows away the pre-washed rubbish.

The Kirb Krawler gets a bit choked up, and the clock is ticking.

the heap, been utterly reliable. They had been driving it around only ten minutes before the start of the competition. It only takes a couple of minutes for them to discover that a whole load of wires have just come apart under the steering column. It's soon running again, but it's a classic *Scrap* irony moment.

On the second start, the Catalysts shoot forward to the centre of the rubbish-covered area and start sucking up grit. As soon as a sheet of newspaper gets near their suction pipe it gets blocked, which means Martin Bremner, their expert, has to undo the pipe, reverse it and un-suck the blockage.

Meanwhile, the Chaos Crew drive slowly across the field of trash and leave a clean trail behind them. From where I'm standing, it looks like an ultra-efficient sweeping machine that will clear the whole area in a couple of minutes.

'Chaos Crew are looking good, Roger,' I say to the judge.

'Yes, but they're not actually picking anything up. They're just bulldozing,' he says; and, of course, he's right. Closer inspection reveals a huge pile of rubbish jammed up against the intake flap of their machine. The paddles are turning, and Spike is on top of the hybrid Land Rover ready to pack trash, but none is coming up.

John and Mike Hasler from the Chaos Crew jump down and start unblocking the machine. When Andy drives forward again, rubbish is finally being dragged up their conveyor belt into the washing machine case they are using to collect it in.

The Catalysts are making a hell of a noise as they continue their erratic journey around the test area. As bits of grit, cans and bottles fly up the pipe, they hit the impeller blades and are shattered, and their remains are flung into the collecting bin they have fashioned out of a cut and folded Transit van.

The half-hour goes fast. Towards the end, the Chaos Crew's conveyor belt is almost torn in two when one of their paddles is ripped off by blocked rubbish. The Catalysts' fan is shaking rather unpleasantly and making more and more noise. In the last minute of the competition, Andy drives the Chaos machine at a much greater speed, and although there are bits falling off all the time, it actually works more efficiently, showering Spike with trash.

By some kind of miracle, both machines actually make it to the end. The Chaos Crew have collected two large sacks of rubbish, and are feeling very proud of their efforts. The Catalysts open the door of their Transit van to

Two big sacks of trash, and the moment of truth.

reveal the rubbish they have collected. I am expecting to see it at least half full, but there's much less inside than I would have thought. I catch a sly grin cross Chaos Andy's face when he sees it. But when the Catalysts dive inside the van and start to scoop it all out, it's clear that it may not have volume, but it has weight.

We are not going to know the outcome until each of the sacks is strapped to the weighing scales I saw Clint making the other day. Dom and John, dressed in white scientists' coats, are acting as the *Scrapheap* marshalls, tying the heavy sacks to the scales. The scales are hanging from a fork-lift truck, which slowly lifts the sacks into the air. There is no argument now – it's immediately apparent who has won...

Inspector Dom and a pair of old pants.

MONSTER TRUCK

I am feeling a little bit bleary as I stumble about the set in the early morning dark. I usually feel very chipper at dawn, following, as I do, a very rigorous fitness regime. I walk at least once a week and I have been known to run; I eat only organic double cheeseburgers, and I love watching other people trying to keep fit. However, one thing I really don't do much is drink alcohol. Until, for some unknown reason, the night before the biggest build that the brains behind *Scrapheap* have ever thrown at the teams.

I went to a cocktail lounge on Sunset Strip in West Hollywood – the Chateau Marmont Bar, where some very interesting Hollywood characters were cruising around. The bar is part of the weird-looking Chateau Marmont Hotel, which is very 'famous' in a Hollywood way, due mainly to the A-list celebs who've popped their clogs while staying as guests.

A large group of off-duty scrappers gathered there and tried out various cocktails. I only needed a sip of mine and I started to wobble, but it tasted very nice. I also 'tried' everyone else's cocktail, which may have been rash for a man of my alcohol *naïveté*.

Robert finding out why they keep him on the other side of the camera.

The hardcore scrappers are mostly people young enough to be my children, who all know an alarming amount about the niceties of cocktails. I bowed out early, walking awkwardly in a pair of pointy-toed cowboy boots I'd bought at a flea market earlier in the day for $20. Maybe this place is really getting to me – I wouldn't be seen dead in footwear like that anywhere else.

The site is bustling when I get there. I'm early and the teams haven't arrived, but something else has. Stretching half the distance of a football pitch is a truck, the like of which could only exist in America. On its side is the immortal phrase 'Big Foot'.

'Bit of a giveaway,' I say to Cathy.

'You'd think so, wouldn't you? But the teams were here yesterday when it arrived, and apparently none of them took any notice.'

More noise and enthusiasm than is quite polite in a scrapyard.

The team bus pulls up and six of the most excitable people I have ever met – well, when hungover – pile out in to the crisp, early morning light. The Abominable Snowmen have travelled the furthest, from a British Antarctic research station. The Mulewrights have come from just up the road (well, plus a few hundred miles) in San Francisco, and everybody is very glad to see them.

On the back wall of the build area is a plan of the competition that Cathy drew during the first day's shoot. There's a series of boxes in a sideways pyramid, and each box represents a round, or programme, in the competition. In today's box are two team names, the Abominable Snowmen and the Barley Pickers, but the Barley Pickers have been crossed out and replaced by the Mulewrights. The Barley Pickers are a team made up of three farmers. They all live on farms in England and in April 2001 restrictions caused by the outbreak of foot and mouth disease in the UK meant they just couldn't come. Director Johanna, who has been very involved with the teams for the previous couple of months, has taken the brunt of this news, but she is an amazingly brave woman who doesn't seem daunted by anything: 'It's all a total mess, just like my life, so I'm used to it, and the Mulewrights are spectacular.'

She's right. The Mulewrights are three engineers and yes, without doubt, they're American and proud of it. They met through the Millwrights and Machinery Erectors Union – they're all proud Union men – and for some reason that still evades me, the Millwrights, ie people who build mills, has been turned into the Mulewrights, clearly not people who build mules.

"I LOVE TO WORK!"

Their captain, Ray Cardiero, is a tightly packed ball of enthusiasm and 'can-do' bravado. Rick Foreman is a big, tall, smiling guy, and it only takes a glance at his engineer's hands to convince you he's a capable guy when it comes to fixing stuff. All around both of them, out of focus for me due to rapid movement, is a jumping bean of a man, someone who literally cannot keep still. Carlos Silvera is expressing his excitement in a highly explosive physical way.

'I am so happy to be here,' he keeps saying as he bounds around, jumping up and down. 'I love this show so much. I am so, so happy to be here!'

'He works very hard,' says Ray, putting a calming hand on Carlos' shoulder. It doesn't calm him.

'I love to work!' says Carlos, 'and I am so happy to be on this show. We love this show, we love it!' He is now flying sideways as well as jumping up and down, his smile broad – one could say crazy, but no, this is just sheer, deep American-blend joy. 'It's what we do all day. I keep a whole bunch of jetways running – you know, the big walkway tubes that come up to the side of a plane when you arrive at an airport terminal. It's us that keeps them going, man, in San Francisco, San Jose and Oakland airports. That's what we do, we fix things in record time. We are so happy to be here. Wow!' Carlos runs around the yard. I don't believe I have ever seen a happier man.

We have all been worrying about the unlikelihood of the Barley Pickers being allowed to leave their farms, let alone the country, and the concern has been that the show will suddenly appear 'too American' if we have an American team on this particular challenge. When I first meet the Mulewrights, I worry that they are going to be so noisy and articulate that they are going to make any low-key English team look rather dull.

MONSTER TRUCK

Luckily, I now have proof that if you shut English engineers in a small building in the Antarctic for long enough, they shed their dourness very rapidly when you let them loose on a scrapheap in the sun – no matter how reserved they are when they go in. Paul Rose, David 'Scooby' Ganiford and Rodney Arnold are as loud, enthusiastic and delighted to be on *Scrapheap* as any English team has ever been. No, more so – they are as crazily energetic as their American opponents. Paul is a wonderfully enthusiastic fellow, his face battered by his working conditions. He's been in the Antarctic the longest, but he's worked with his team very closely for the last four years.

'We're like a three-headed monster,' he enthuses. 'And we're just totally over the top about this, we're going to have such a brilliant time here.'

Such a huge level of enthusiasm from both teams is very reassuring, because what we are asking these teams to do today is pushing the engineering insanity envelope to the very, very limit.

Although it is still cool at 7.00am, anyone can tell that this build is going to be a warmie. It's the first truly hot day since we've been in LA, and the sky is as clear as a baby's skin. By the time the build actually starts at about 9.30am, it's already very, very warm. Those not used to the tempera-ture – like, say, a team from the Antarctic – could already find it very hot.

I am really looking forward to telling them what they've got to make, I'm really looking forward to watching them make it, and I'm really, really looking forward to seeing them test these babies: 'Teams, your challenge today is to build a vehicle capable of racing over the gargantuan obstacles of our swervin' dirt track, crushing a few cars along the way. Yes, you've got to build a Monster Truck!'

The teams' reaction is phenomenal. Sometimes we have to do the introduction

A little behind the scenes 'help' in the monster truck department.

The Mules go straight for the really big wheel...

... and oh! So do the Snowmen.

again to get the teams to react, but not today. They bounce off the trash with excitement. They're jumping up and down and cheering so much that Cathy has to wait until they calm down before she can explain the rules of the challenge.

So, they have to build a monster truck. If you have to ask 'What the hell is that?' join the club. It is a very American phenomenon: a pick-up truck with an absurdly powerful engine and even more absurdly huge wheels that can 'go over anything'. We don't need to explain a thing to either team. They are so on the ball about this, so up for it, and busting their chops to get started.

Once in their build areas they start their team chats and immediately, as I listen to the Abominable Snowmen, I hear the term 'big' being used a lot. Everything about this build is going to be big. In fact Tim Barks, the Snowmen's expert, is not only working out a design for the machine they are going to build, he's drawing a plan of where they'll put the components. Everything they use will be so big, they could easily run out of space.

The other word they use a great deal, together with big, is 'block'. 'Big block' refers to the engine they will be using – a big block Chevy, or a big block Ford. I've checked with Tristan, John and Todd from the engineering department, and there are three big block engines buried on the site, all of them large-capacity V8s. For the benefit of non-V8-obsessive people, these are very big and extremely heavy engines. The average family car has a 1.2 to 1.8-litre engine with 50-80 horsepower. These big fellows are around 7 litres with about 250 horsepower. Then, when they are tuned up and supercharged like the one in the dragster driven by Smax Smith in the last series, they can produce 3,500 horsepower. That's a lot of horses – a silly number really. Smax Smith goes from a standing start to 300 miles an hour in about five seconds. All that big block boy thrill aside, 250 horsepower is enough to break things like drive shafts and axles and possibly other things that are more important, like people.

The two experts are both monster truck builders and drivers from England. With the Abominable Snowmen is Tim Barks, a sensitive-looking individual who, if you walked past him in the street, wouldn't make you immediately think 'monster truck driver'. He is the technical director of the European Monster Truck Racing Association, and I never even knew there was one. I'm learning a lot. Tim built his own monster truck from scratch using things like axles from mobile cranes, a nitro-methane-powered big block engine and specially constructed shock absorbers and suspension. The result is a huge, oversized vehicle that can not only climb steep hills, jump over cars and float on water, but can out-accelerate a Ferrari up to 60mph, even on grass. He clearly knows his stuff, and the Snowmen are impressed.

Tim's design is simple: get a big truck, maybe a military vehicle, cut off the bodywork, adapt the transmission and fit in a big block engine. Then bolt on some enormous wheels, maybe from a tractor or massive earth-mover, then throw on the body of a pick-up truck to make it look vaguely like a truck. In fact the only thing he mentions that doesn't start with the words massive, big, or heavy is the steering wheel. Apparently, that can be normal.

Surely they can't be serious.

On the Mulewrights' team, expert Nigel Morris is a different-looking monster truck guy. In fact, if you walked past him on the street you would probably think, 'Now he is a monster truck driver.' Nigel is a big fellow, as Eloise, the costume queen, found out. Within moments of the start of the challenge, he had managed to rip open the trouser leg of his heavy-duty overalls. A quick bit of off-camera stitching soon solved the problem and Nigel was back in the thick of it.

He runs a company called LA Supertrux in Daventry and makes custom four-wheel drive cars – he recently made one for Shane from Boyzone. The Mulewrights love Nigel, and they jump up and down, screaming and shouting with joy as he describes what he thinks they should build together. In contrast to Tim on the other side of the wall, Nigel wants to build a chassis from scratch. Other than that, the word 'big' is again liberally used to describe everything.

When the scavengers leave the build area, both drivers prove to be incredibly adept at controlling the six-wheel drive buggies. They spin them around, bounce them over bits of metal debris and come so close to crashing that it looks like they actually have, but then they appear out of a cloud of dust a moment later, unscathed. Cathy and I watch in non-mock horror at the speed and insanity of their enthusiasm. Camera operators dive for cover; it's dangerous out there in deep scrap land.

Very quickly, some monstrously big stuff is being dragged into the build areas, most of it so big the little buggies can't possibly move it. Technician 'Jesus' John is

Mulewright Rick doing what he loves to do: 'Work!'

discreetly brought in with a very big fork-lift to push the heavy chassis. Both teams get his assistance, so it's not really cheating – or at least it's cheating that's fair to both teams. The Abominable Snowmen seem to start to work immediately, oxy-acetylene torches spitting and hissing their way through heavy steel beams.

The Mulewrights start hacking great lumps out of the chassis they have scavenged. They're removing the transfer box – the secondary gearbox that will drive the front and rear wheels.

Backstage, the technical crew and the experts (including the daddy of monster truck racing, Bob Chandler) are looking a little concerned about this plan. They have all agreed that it is possible to build a rudimentary monster truck in ten hours – just. But they were thinking along the lines of using existing pieces, not building a very complicated chassis from scratch. They also know that there isn't enough material of the sort the Mulewrights need in the yard. After the minor embarrassments of the pile of new steel box section found by the egg-launcher teams, and the impeller blade found by the Catalysts, a very close watch has been kept on what's in the yard and what isn't.

'THEY ARE VERY STUFFED'

'There's nothing they need in there,' says Tristan with a hint of pleasure. 'They are very stuffed.'

But a glance over the wall tells us that the Mulewrights aren't bothered they're still looking for heavy-duty steel bars and tubing to make their chassis.

I talk to Jim Kramer, our judge for the day. What a charmer – this man can talk on camera with no trouble at all. Jim has been driving monster trucks since 1982. He can jump them, bounce them around, and when it goes a bit wrong, roll them over. But not roll them over on their side like any normal person would roll over a wheeled vehicle; he rolls them over the front end, on to the roof, then over the back end and on to the wheels again.

Jim has just handed in his monster truck driving licence because although, as he assures me, the technology surrounding the driver makes him very safe, when you jump a truck high into the air, it's very painful for the driver when it comes back down to earth.

When Jim and I have finished, I glance into the Mulewrights' build area. It's disappeared under a massive tyre showroom. They have scavenged five or six tractor tyres and three utterly vast spheres of carved rubber that are only vaguely tyre-like. They have hardly any room to walk, let alone build anything.

'It's going to be big,' says Jim, who is clearly enjoying himself.

Lunch is very pleasant today, sitting in the shade of one of the only three oak trees for miles. You couldn't call Pendleton Street a cosy, suburban neighbourhood,

Nigel and the Mules check for punctures.

but it's a very welcome break from the noise and dust of the build areas. The teams, of course, are still in there, but they are eating and even Carlos is sitting down.

I sit next to James Brighton, an engineering consultant who has been on the show before. He was the genius behind the slowest-moving machine ever built by human beings, the walking machine built by Bowser and co, which appeared in the final of Series Two.

James and director Johanna Gibbon have just come back from doing a location recce for an upcoming challenge of major insanity, as always. They have been in Nevada, where they hired a Dodge Viper, a car with an 8-litre V10 engine, which is capable of getting from 0 to 60 in 4.1 seconds. The obvious choice, I would say, when choosing a hire car in a country with a speed limit of 65mph – choose one that can easily achieve 150mph. They were cruising around on the fringes of Las Vegas when the car broke down. Of *course* it broke down – it was distantly connected with *Scrapheap*; they know about these things, cars. The local garage couldn't fix it, and the company they hired the car from couldn't fix it. Some sort of delicate electronics had thrown a wobbly, and nothing worked. James is not the sort of man to leave complex machinery idle – he's used to *Scrapheap*, for goodness' sake. So as soon as all other options had been removed, he was in there with his screwdriver and Leatherman. As it was getting dark, a state patrolman drew up and Jamie explained he needed to fix the car, but he couldn't see – he needed a torch. The officer got a little alarmed, thinking Jamie was some British nutter who had stolen the car and wanted to burn it. In the US, a torch can only mean a stick with flames at one end; to see in the dark the American way, you need a flashlight. I can see by the look on Johanna's face that she actually enjoyed being driven around the desert in a ludicrous-looking sports car that could 'burn rubber' in all six gears.

After lunch, the Snowmen have their engine fitted and are working on their transmission. These guys work very fast – maybe it's a habit from working outside in -30° temperatures; you don't want to hang about too long. They are nearly ready to start up their engine and test their transmission, which they've also completely rebuilt.

Now, I can't tell you exactly why I love the sound of a *Scrapheap* V8 engine (especially a very big V8 engine) when it starts up, but I do. I wouldn't miss it for the world. As the Snowmen started to fiddle with their big block, I am hovering around outside, waiting to dash in to be on hand when they fire it up. They connect the battery and I'm in there, soon joined by Cathy. Scooby holds two wires together while Tim pours some petrol into the carburettor – it all looks highly dangerous, but they seem to know what they're doing and the engine bursts into life immediately. When you stand very near a 7-litre V8 that has no exhaust pipes or silencers, it is very, very noisy. It's a gut-churning, primal roar. Somehow, mankind has managed to fabricate something with the visceral passion and eagerness of a wild cat. It actually hurts my eyes when Tim flips the throttle. Angry yellow flames spit out of the stubby exhaust manifold. I know, intellectually, that it's just a bunch of pistons going up and down, driven by a series of small explosions contained in a cylinder. I know that, but what I

feel is something else – a mixture of terror and awe at the lazy power of this lump of steel. It's not showing off, it's not like a racy four-cylinder engine that can rev really fast and is fuel-efficient and clean-burning. This is an overweight, gas-guzzling bear. It doesn't give a damn what you think, it's going to make a lot of noise and create a lot of pollution but deliver a huge amount of torque, and is more than happy to drive this oversized monstrosity the team are building. And drive it over anything.

Tim and the Abominable Snowmen aboard their insane creation.

'That was loud,' says Cathy. She's grown to love V8s too, after claiming to be completely oblivious to their attraction when we started making *Scrapheap Challenge* four years ago. She is now seriously considering buying a bright yellow 1956 Ford pick-up powered by a 320 cubic inch V8 – not exactly a big block, but a very large block by any standards. And for a 'lady driver', as she refers to herself, just the job.

Anyway, all the Snowmen have to do now is adapt the three tractor tyres they've found, which are all slightly different sizes, and find a fourth, then bolt them to the axles. When I say that's all they have to do, technically it's a little more complex, of course. The bolt-holes in the wheels of the tractor tyres are designed to fit on a tractor, not a military truck. They have to cut out the centre of the tractor wheels and weld the centre of the truck tyres in their place. That's the theory and it sounds horribly difficult; captain Paul is clearly having second thoughts, but they are up against it since they don't have the right tyres. The Mulewrights seemed to clear the yard of tyres in moments.

Over the other side of the wall, things are not going quite so smoothly. Team expert Nigel has finally admitted defeat. They just can't build a chassis from scratch in the time allotted. They have had to make a violent U-turn and use the old truck chassis they have just finished cutting to pieces.

With less than five hours to go, they somehow manage to galvanize themselves into action to catch up. The sun is now brutally hot. When I sit on the throne, there is a ten-second period of pain as my backside gets used to the feeling of being in close contact with vinyl heated to flesh-scorching temperatures.

Not quite the same as changing the wheel on your family hatchback...

The Mulewrights work like, well, Mulewrights, welding the structure back together, mounting an equally enormous engine and re-fabricating their previously dismembered running gear. Within a couple of hours they have not only caught up with the Snowmen in terms of

build, they have overtaken them. Their enormous tyres will just bolt on with no need to adapt them, a task that is slowing the Snowmen down considerably.

Backstage, the venerable Clint is building some scrap starting lights for the upcoming monster truck race. Cathy and I get a sneak preview of Bob Chandler's 'Big Foot', which is inside the enormous truck parked outside the gates on Pendleton Street. As we stand in the cavernous interior of the wheeled container, the high-tech beast towers over us, and it's only wearing its carpet slippers. In order to fit the oversized creation in the truck, they have to remove the massive tyres and replace them with little tractor tyres. Well, they look little in comparison with the massive things that it's fitted with normally.

On camera at the back of the set, Cathy asks me, 'Why? Why do men want to make and drive these absurd creations?' I am a little at a loss to explain. My best shot is that it comes from a desire to have something bigger and louder than anyone else. Also, there is a fascination with big tyres and they way they grip and bounce, which could be Freudian but I don't see how, and frankly I don't care. Maybe it's something to do with the American psyche – wanting to make something awe-inspiring, loud and, ultimately, purely for show. Monster trucks use technology and engineering for showbiz. What else can you do in them but show off? Getting shopping in the back would be very hard, as the back is about ten feet up in the air.

As the sun finally falls and the temperature drops rapidly towards very cold, the teams struggle away like men possessed. And they are – possessed by the monsters that are beginning to tower above them. The Mulewrights' protective roll bars have been shaped out of new steel tubing, using amazing hydraulic pipe benders. They're not going to bother attaching a body, as there's no time. The Snowmen mount their pick-up truck body and weld it on like it's a trophy on top of a huge coffee table that just happens to be fitted with four massive tractor tyres. I have never seen anything this big built on *Scrapheap Challenge*. The machines take up the entire build area,

The Mules and their amazing giant roller skate.

which makes recording them on camera increasingly difficult.

During the day, we had two accidents for the first time I can remember. One was serious. Jamie Budge, the American stills photographer, fractured his ankle. He fell over while trying to get the huge machine in focus. Andy, one of the English camera operators who has worked on dozens of *Scrapheap* and *Junkyard War* challenges, had the same accident but thankfully was less seriously hurt. He bruised his coccyx and, as he told me later, his pride. The camera operators on the show have a really difficult task, not only staying out of each others' shots and avoiding the dangers of very enthusiastic engineers, but looking through an eyepiece as they negotiate their way around a chaotic mess of bits of metal, tools and general rubbish. How more of them haven't come a cropper is nothing short of miraculous.

In the closing moments of the build, I think of all the people who've been in the show who would have loved this challenge. It's so big and noisy, there is so much welding and cutting going on, and the engines are the biggest we've ever used. I think of Bowser, Colonel Strawbridge, the Chemical Brothers, the Chaos Crew, the Megalomaniacs. They would all have dived in and made something amazing, but these two teams that we've never met before have done everyone proud: 'OK, teams, your time is up!'

Even now, after ten hours of fantastically hard work, the cheer goes up. The teams run around looking at each others' machines. They don't hear anyone say, 'It's a wrap, go home.'

'Hey, that is awesome!' screams Carlos when he sees the Snowmen's machine. Indeed it is. It really looks like a proper monster truck – a funny little pick-up sitting above four enormous tyres. During the last couple of hours, the teams did a bit of bartering, swapping tyres they didn't need for ones they did.

I notice experts Nigel and Tim congratulating each other warmly. They are old mates from the monster truck fraternity, both in awe at the presence of the father of the sport, Bob Chandler, who enters the build areas for a closer look.

'Good job, guys,' says Bob. 'Good job.'

From the looks on Nigel and Tim's faces, this is praise indeed.

The Test

The weather here has been a bit of a surprise. On all my previous visits to Southern California it's been bright, sunny and warm. Always, every day. When we arrive at the Ventura Raceway, which is about 60 miles west of Hollywood, right on the beach, it's actually cold. It's a little fresh, it's very foggy and the mountains we drove past on the way have disappeared behind a blanket of thick sea mist. 'Maybe it's to do with global warming,' I say to Rey Vincenti, our increasingly smiling first assistant director.

'Maybe not,' he replies. 'Maybe it's to do with you English guys bringing your stinking weather with you.'

Rey doesn't say much, but what he does say usually packs a punch. Rey has a military background; he was a soldier in Vietnam in 1969, when he was

'OF COURSE, I COULD TELL YOU, BUT THEN I'D HAVE TO KILL YOU'

just nineteen years old. No one, especially all the women on the crew, can believe he's old enough to have been there. Even I can do the maths, he's fifty-one but looks thirty-five, with dark and still annoyingly thick Italian-American hair. He is a very well-groomed man with strong, well-kept hands that he gently massages together as he speaks. I ask him about his time in 'Nam, and like most people I've ever spoken to about it, he just says ominously, 'There's a lot of stuff I couldn't tell you.'

'Sure, sure,' I twitter nervously.

This is usually followed by the quip, 'Of course, I could tell you, but then I'd have to kill you' – a favourite of Colonel Strawbridge of the Brothers in Arms team. But Rey is different.

Faster than a Ferrari, noisier than a thrash metal band... here's Bigfoot.

He continues, '...unless you bought me a whole load of beers. Then I'd tell you everything.' He smiles. It's slightly hard to read his face, as he's wearing mirrored sunglasses that only allow me to see a small version of how he sees me. 'Of course, I might have a flashback and take you out,' he adds, then pats me on the back to reassure me. 'Can we have you on set, please, Robert – five-hour time check coming up.'

The morning is spent doing a few pieces to camera on the giant dirt track that makes up the oceanside Ventura Raceway. The course for the monster truck challenge is almost complete. Four humpy jumps of piled dirt, and a row of five scrap cars with a dirt ramp at either end. A digger is still busy near me, clearly quite a noisy operation; but not noisy enough, it seems. Suddenly there is another noise, a far deeper growl that makes the earth shake beneath our feet. It's coming from behind the large concrete stands at one side of the track and we can hear it above the sound of the digger, which is all of six feet away.

'They've fired up Big Foot,' says Dom as he skids to a halt on the six-wheeler. He is grinning almost manically. 'Badda bing, badda boom!'

Some builders are erecting new stands at one side of the course. They're already about twelve feet high, but suddenly I can see a blue roof moving along the other side of the structure.

'Oh, my God,' says Cathy, who has run across the dirt to join the little gaggle of directors and camera operators who are huddling in fear at one side. 'That is so noisy.'

Indeed it is. It's painfully noisy as it rumbles towards us. $200,000 worth of high-tech, nitro-methane-powered monster truck. The latest in a 25-year-long line of similar machines, this one is presently at the cutting edge of the technology. Judge Jim has already told me it's about to be surpassed by a new, even more powerful machine.

The driver of the vehicle, Dave Harkey, steers the huge machine to the far end of the circuit and turns it around. With a suddenness that leaves my ears ringing, the engine dies and silence falls. The driver appears from underneath the truck, there are no doors, just a hole in the floor because the floor is so high above the ground.

I then get involved in a complex discussion with Cathy and Johanna as to how to shoot the opening sequence for the new series. Cathy has to say 'Welcome back to *Scrapheap Challenge*. We've got new teams, new machines...' at which point Johanna wants the two-ton monster truck to fly past Cathy and land on the cars right behind her. We don't know how dangerous it is, and how close Cathy can stand to the truck's impact point.

'I'll show you,' says driver Dave, with a friendly grin.

He climbs back into his cab and we all stand back. Now, I've seen dragsters, tanks and very fast cars in action. I've even sat in them and in some cases had a little drive, but I have never seen anything like this. For a monster truck groupie, this would be run-of-the-mill fare – but for us, standing so close, it's nothing short of miraculous.

This thing, this monster noise-maker, stands on the dirt rumbling in its own very loud way, when suddenly what was already very loud becomes truly deafening as the supercharger pumps in gallons of methyl-alcohol fuel and the dormant shape bursts into life. Over twenty feet it builds up enough speed to launch itself into the air by going up a pile of dirt no bigger than the average suburban rockery. It seems to fly, defying logic, defying gravity, it defies every law of sense I have ever known.

'It's bloody amazing!' says Cathy. She had initially been scared about standing too close to the launch point for this stunt, but that's all changed. 'I want to lie underneath as it goes over,' she says.

Rey glances at me. He is still trying to differentiate between our jokes and serious comments. His look says, 'She's crazy, right – if you want, I'll ring the funny farm.'

The monster truck behaves itself and completes a series of jumps right behind Cathy, who's facing the **"IT'S BLOODY AMAZING!"** camera and is unable to see what is happening, but is very able to hear. Johanna is very pleased with the shot. Normally quite expressive, she just stands with wide eyes and slack jaw: 'Wow'.

Robert is convinced the viewers will believe he was allowed to drive this thing.

However, I'm a little disappointed, because although I am now clambering into the fireproof suit that driver Dave Harkey was wearing and then struggling up into the driving compartment of the monster truck, I won't actually get to drive it. It may look like I do on the telly, because I add the tag-line to Cathy's introduction as though it's me driving the flying truck behind her.

This is how the script looks:

Cathy: 'Welcome back to *Scrapheap Challenge*, we've got new teams, new machines…'

A monster truck jumps over a row of cars behind Cathy, lands and comes to a stop. Robert leans out of the window and takes off his helmet.

Robert: '…and a brand new motor.'

As I say the line, half the crew are hanging on to either end of Big Foot, rocking it up and down to make it look as though it's just stopped. I could have lied to you and told you I did drive it and make it jump, but I know I would have been found out.

Johanna wants some footage of Big Foot in action to cut into the show and explain what it is the teams are trying to make, so Dave gets back into his fireproof suit and starts up. So far, we have seen the way this thing can jump, and how fast it can accelerate, but we didn't know quite how wild it can get. As the massive engine screams, Big Foot lurches forward and starts to rocket around the circuit. I am standing with a small crowd of open-mouthed scrappers by the emergency exit, and as Big Foot powers around the corner towards us, many people flee. It's skidding sideways, looking totally out of control, and we don't know enough about it to know if this is what's meant to happen. I am frozen to the spot. I've never seen anything so big move so fast and make so much noise while doing it. Eventually, Dave takes a tight turn at the far end of the circuit and heads towards us. The front wheels hit an earth mound and fly up into the air, but instead of dropping back down again as they have done previously, the truck stays in that position and accelerates.

It's coming straight at us, chassis first. I can clearly see the drive shafts spinning as the front tyres are 25 feet in the air, and the noise is genuinely traumatic. Dave Harkey is sitting in the driving seat facing the sky. He has to steer by looking through the floor, which is made of Perspex, but how on earth he actually steers is a mystery. At the last minute he veers off to one side and the front wheels make thundering contact with the earth again.

'Now you know what awesome means,' says Rey Vincenti.

'You're not kidding,' says Cathy. 'That was terrifying, but I understand monster trucks now. They're bloody brilliant.'

Throughout this time, the teams have been undertaking what we have decided to refer to as 'heavy tinkering'. They are always allowed an hour or so of 'tinker time' on the day of the challenge, to make any last-minute adjustments. This time, however, their tinkering is of a slightly more complex nature. By the end of the build day, neither team had much in the way of steering control. The Mulewrights had a steering wheel, but it didn't do anything, just spun in the breeze. The Abominable Snowmen had a steering wheel connected to the steering assembly, but it would take four genuine abominable snowmen to turn it. With no power-assisted steering, turning two tractor wheels weighing 500 pounds each that are supporting three-quarters of a ton of machinery requires quite a bit of force to be applied. So the 'heavy tinkering' session is allowing the teams to make their vehicles steerable – a fairly desirable attribute for all of us.

The challenge starts after lunch. Because of the undeniably dangerous nature of the race, the two experts, Nigel and Tim, will be driving their teams' trucks. Discussion has taken place during the build and at various

Some serious 'tinker time' for the Snowmen.

production meetings about the possibility of a head-to-head race. But the trucks have little in the way of brakes, and what can confidently be classified as rudimentary steering; so the decision is taken to race them one after the other. The one with the fastest time wins.

Off-camera, judge Jim tosses a silver dollar. Snowmen team captain Paul calls heads, but it's tails. Nigel Morris is going first in the Mulewrights' *Mad Max*-style machine. I stand next to Big Foot with Jim as we watch Nigel take a rolling start. The big beast takes a bit of moving from a standstill, and the teams have agreed that this is a fair method to get going.

The truck is moving well. Not amazingly fast, but it's going steady. As it goes over the earth mounds it behaves very differently to Big Foot. This is mainly due to its total lack of rear suspension – both machines have kept the front suspension from the original military vehicles, but their rear axles are welded directly to the chassis. As it slams over the mounds, it looks much like when you drop a lump of concrete on to a very hard floor. There's not a lot of give. Nigel takes the first bend at a good speed, gently goes up the earth mound and over the cars as if it were a neat little bridge. No trouble at all. He takes the last bend a little faster and 'makes air' as he goes over the last jump. The front wheels leave the ground, but the back wheels slam into the dirt with a bone-shaking thump.

The Polar Monster sails over the obstacles.

He completed the circuit in 49.51 seconds. In the distance I can see Carlos from the Mulewrights flying into the air with delight. It's a challenge to Tim, who quickly suits up and clambers into the Snowmen's monster truck.

Tim takes a slightly different route around the course, which I later discover is due to their 'delayed response' steering system. It's a special new design the team has come up with for this challenge. It means that when

Tim moves the steering wheel, he has to wait a couple of seconds for the giant tractor wheels beneath him to move in response. Amazingly he sticks to the course very well and the machine holds up, coming in at an astounding 49.40 seconds. It amazes Jim and I how two vehicles made of old scrap and driven by two different drivers can end up coming so close.

The Mules machine in carpet slippers...

There is a delay before the Mulewrights can go again as their brake pedal fell off during the first run, but Ray and the team soon fix it. Nigel sets off, and again the truck crunches over the bumps. This time I watch Nigel as opposed to the truck, and I can see that he really bangs down after each jump. There is nothing like a shock absorber, or even a very soft seat to protect him, and he's a big lad.

'That has got to hurt,' I say to Jim.

'Yep, it sure will.'

... and with its outdoor boots on.

After another faultless run, Nigel turns in a time of 49.72 seconds, slightly slower than his first run. He's not pleased. He claims the engine is running like 'a bag of washing' but there is nothing the team can do now. It's make-or-break time.

Tim starts out on the Snowmen's second run and anyone can see he is going a hell of a lot faster, but his delayed response steering seems to be steering him directly at judge Jim, the cameraman Jacob who can't see any of this, and me. Jacob can tell by our faces that our terror is becoming very real. I can see his eyes flicker as we describe how close this enormous, noisy, unsteerable machine is getting to us. Somehow, just in time, Tim manages to wrestle the beast around the corner and over the cars, much faster this time. He takes the back straight so fast the rear wheels are skidding around, kicking up dust. That has to be the fastest yet.

I check Jim's stopwatch: 50.32 seconds. I can't believe it. The Snowmen can't believe it. It was slower, and yet it looked faster. How could it be? Jim thinks that because of the steering, Tim is taking all the corners much wider than Nigel and therefore travelling a greater distance around the track. They're clever, these monster truck men.

Nigel walks back across the course and clambers up for the third and final run. As it stands, the Snowmen are in the lead by a tenth of a second; they still have the fastest time. Nigel knows that this is it. He's going to thrash it – either the machine will break to bits, or he'll shave something off that time and win the competition.

He starts the engine and we all get ready. Then the engine stalls and there's a moment's silence; when he's strapped into his chair, he can't reach the starter switch. After a couple of seconds I see Clint run around the vehicle and press the switch. The engine starts first time and Clint legs it back to the starting lights control position. This time Nigel gets off to an impressive start, taking the first two jumps faster than ever and coming down really heavily on the other side. The machine holds up. He negotiates the first corner a little wider than before but much, much faster. He almost flies over the row of scrap cars as if they were a smooth road, the machine's giant tyres are coping with the bumpy ride, he's down the other side now and flying around the last bend. The truck's V8 is screaming, flames are visible from the exhaust port as Nigel keeps the pedal to the metal.

But something's wrong. Just before he reaches the final jumps he backs off. I can see that he's lost concentration, and yet everything sounds fine, the engine is still roaring; but he is holding on to the roll cage above his head. He hits the last earth mound hard, the front wheels again leave the dirt and I can see Nigel badly buffeted in his seat. As he rolls past us he seems to be holding up both hands in the air in victory. He should be. The new time is ten seconds faster than Tim – an incredible improvement.

Then, as the engine dies, I hear the fateful words from Nigel: 'I'm hurt.'

Within seconds, the car is crawling with men. Tim is first up, standing on the roll cage above Nigel asking where he hurts. It's clearly his back; he's pulling up on the roll cage trying to relieve the pain. Ray Cordeiro is up behind Nigel, holding his head, and the medics, who have been hiding off the circuit, come running up. As Cathy joins me there can be no doubt that this is serious. This is our worst nightmare. We have been so fortunate on *Scrapheap* to have been so amazingly accident-free. The most serious incident to date was when Babs Munsen, Bowser's wife, turned over the mileage marathon vehicle and it landed on her arm. She didn't break a bone – due mainly, I think, to the fact that Babs is one very tough lady – but she did damage the muscle and still has a bit of trouble with it to this day. But we have never had anything like this. It's horrific.

The safety crew start peeling away the roll cage away with hydraulic cutters, Ray holding Nigel's head steady while the medic fits him with a neck brace. I turn to Cathy who is very upset and close to tears. She has had enough medical training to know what a back injury can mean. As we watch in frozen horror, I can see that Nigel is moving his feet. I point this out to Cathy and ask if that means he's not paralyzed. She confirms that this means whatever injury has been caused is not as serious as it might be. However, we have to deal with the situation in a way that assumes the worst.

After five minutes, the roll cage is cut off and Nigel is manhandled on to a stretcher, raised high on a fork-lift truck. He is lowered to the ground and I can see his face; he's holding his eyes shut with one hand, clearly in a great deal of pain. Jeremy Cross appears, ashen-faced; no jokes are flying around about this. A lot of people are on phones, another ambulance arrives and more paramedics appear as Nigel is carried into the ambulance. Tim climbs in with him. He wants to go to hospital with his friend. No one is thinking of the competition or the show, the whole thing has come to a sickening halt. After a while, Tim emerges, now very red-eyed.

We gather around to see what will transpire. Tim smiles a little: 'Nigel says only a total bastard wouldn't complete the race. He wants me to go ahead.'

A discussion ensues between Jeremy, Cathy and Peter Clews, who has been on the phone constantly. Johanna the director joins us and we talk about what to do. No one really feels like carrying on, except Tim. We watch the ambulance drive away and realize that it's far too much to load on the poor guy. His best mate has just gone to hospital with heaven-knows-what wrong with his back, and we're all looking at this charming, modest young man to see if we can finish a TV show. The whole thing feels skewed, but all Tim asks for is half an hour and a cup of tea in order to find his feet.

Somehow, after coffee, tea and doughnuts, the whole crew starts to calm down. People are beginning to relax, although no one really dares say anything to Tim in case they upset him. We don't want to put any pressure on him to complete the challenge; but on the other hand, we are standing there with only three-quarters of a show. There were obviously no cameras running as the teams and crew cut Nigel out of the monster truck – some of the camera operators were helping, so we have no record of it, and we wouldn't want to include it if we did. I discover that Rick Foreman from the Mulewrights tore his hand open as he tried to wrench off the roll cage. He refused to go to hospital, and although I didn't see it close to, I was assured it was only a surface cut. The teams stand around Tim talking quietly about what they think may have happened to cause Nigel's injury. It seems his safety harness had come undone, which clearly shouldn't have happened.

Tim himself is quiet but calm, sitting on the crash wall at the side of the track, sipping his tea. Then something special happens, something I know I could never

The one and only Ms Rogers awaits the winner.

have done. Cathy moves in and sits on the wall beside Tim and says, in a manner that is beautifully timed to pop the tension, 'How are you then, you crazy mad f**cker?'

Tim laughs, and so does everyone else. Cathy can have quite a colourful turn of phrase off-camera, and this time she uses it to wonderful effect. Maybe her medical training allows her to be less sentimental than most; whatever it is, it's worked. Both teams look at Cathy in admiration. Even though I'm loathe to admit it, with her being my co-host and all (and my boss on the show), Cathy is a bit of a one-off.

'OK, let's do it then,' says Tim; and off he goes for the third and final run of what has turned out to be the biggest and most dramatic *Scrapheap Challenge* I can remember…

Later...

In a huge bar in Burbank, half the crew and the teams sit around a giant table doing what crews and teams talk and dream about a great deal. They are having a beer, and although they are mostly from the UK and this is an American bar, no one is complaining. It's

The teams, sans Nigel, celebrate with bubbly.

true that American beer is very weak, which I have to say I like, because I can't drink very much proper English beer without falling over. But for lads, big strong engineering lads from the Antarctic, well, they need proper man's beer. But this place is a micro-brewery stocking their own range of very nice – and in some cases very strong – beer. The Mulewrights and the Abominable Snowmen are still very noisy. They have had a great time, and apart from Nigel's incident, everything is fine. Cathy gets a call on her mobile, and we discover that Nigel is going to have a CAT scan because they've detected a fracture in a vertebrae and want to do further investigations.

We pass around photographs that the Snowmen team have taken at their base in Antarctica. It's amazing – an overwhelming landscape of rock, ice and very cold-looking water.

Cathy gets another call. It seems that the doctors at the Ventura hospital have decided that the fracture to Nigel's spine is a very old injury. It's been exacerbated by the impacts he experienced doing the test. There is nothing seriously wrong with him and he's free to leave. By the time this news reaches me, everyone is cheering because there, walking through the door and looking, it has to be said, a little stiff in the mid-section, is the man himself.

'If you lot think I'd miss the post-race booze-up, you can all get stuffed,' he said. Or words to that effect.

SNOWMOBILE

Dark and cold, wet and windy. It's not how any of us who don't live here expected California to be. Even for the people who do live here, it's a bit grim.

'Just like home,' comments Rey Vincenti as I arrive. He's dressed for the occasion, a walking mound of windproof, waterproof and coldproof clothing.

The teams for this challenge are the McKarnow Clan from Scotland, and the Ellivators from London. Not as initially noisy as the previous teams, but great fun once I start speaking to them. However, the weather makes it hard to be quite as sparky and up as we should be.

'OK EVERYBODY, BADDA FREAKIN' BING, LET'S DO IT.'

One good side-effect of this cold, grey atmosphere is that everyone wants to get the job done, or to use the vernacular: 'OK everybody, badda freakin' bing, let's do it.'

This morning, the delays the teams normally experience before the build starts are much shorter than usual. The lack of sun means there is an electrician with Cathy and I wherever we go, holding a battery powered 'sun gun', a very powerful little light that gets pointed right at you whenever you're on camera. Andy Calvert is the last remaining English camera operator on the crew, and he is on C camera. This is the one that stays with Cathy and myself for the entire day. The camera crews are split into two groups, A and B, and they work in rotation with one of the teams each over the day.

I've learned that it's worth getting to know the camera operator well, as during the noise and chaos of the build, it's sometimes hard to make out if someone has said 'action' into your earpiece. I rely on Andy to utter something like, 'I have speed, in your own time.' When he says 'speed', he means that the camera is literally up to speed and the recording mechanism is running smoothly. If we start talking as soon as the little red light on the top of the camera comes on, the picture tends to be a bit wibbly and unusable. We have to wait a couple of seconds and, because of the nature of the show, this tiny delay can be very frustrating – it's always during that brief moment that someone will start a grinder right next to us and anything we say will be lost in the din.

Cathy contemplates her creation.

After the last challenge, at first glance this one seems a bit simpler. Not as big, not as noisy, and we're all walking around under the illusion that the teams will throw the machines together and badda bing, job done. You'd think we'd learn, but no.

The McKarnow clan: fresh-faced and ready for anything.

'Teams, you'd better wrap up warm, because we're heading for the hills. And once we're there, we'll need to get around. Your challenge today is to build a jumping, ice-cracking, scrap-challenging snowmobile!'

Gratifyingly, the teams look at one another and cheer under their breath. Not the ear-splitting, jumping-up-and-down madness of the previous challenge, but it's good enough for me.

I am not ashamed to admit that I know more about quantum theory or rare tropical fish breeding than I do about snowmobiles. I have never been skiing – in fact, I haven't seen snow in ten years. We don't get much any more in the UK, and I've spent a lot of winters on the other side of the planet in Australia, anyway. As far as I know, snowmobiles are like a cross between a motorbike and a bread bin that you sit on while chasing James Bond down a hill, firing a machine gun. I've never seen one in real life and have no idea how they work.

Therefore, as I listen to Dave Patterson's soft Scottish accent describing to the McKarnow Clan what he wants them to build, I'm on a steep learning curve. They are going to get a motorbike, take off the wheels, replace the front one with a ski and the rear one with a sort of conveyor belt with teeth, powered by the engine which, in theory, will ride along the surface of the snow and propel them along. David explains to the team (who, although from Scotland, sound about as ignorant of the whole snowmobile thing as I am) that the important thing about snowmobiles is weight and traction. Too heavy and they just sink in; not enough traction and they slide about without moving forwards. It all sounds horribly complicated.

Over on the Ellivators' build area a similar conversation is going on, again with a team that is very familiar with motorbikes but not snowmobiles. Their expert, Micke Nordstrum, is a quietly spoken Swede who has travelled alarmingly fast on a snowmobile. Like, 140mph fast. Where do these people come from, and how come all this high-speed snow-based activity has been taking place in remote and obviously very cold places without me knowing about it? Where have I been all this time?

Once the teams have finished their discussions and the scavengers have set off into the yard to find what they need, I retire behind the scenes feeling a little confused. It's my own fault, of course; due to the hectic schedule we are working to, I have really only just recovered from the monster truck ordeal and I haven't read the script, looked at the notes, checked the tech specs or even learned the names of the teams. I am an unprofessional lazy pig-dog who deserves to be shot. I say this to Cathy as we sip coffee from styrofoam cups and, of course, she agrees with me. She has been working very hard in the LA office of RDF Media, the company behind *Scrapheap Challenge*. She has been to pitch meetings and answered millions of frantic e-mails all day the day before, and yet she has also read the script, knows the names of both teams, the judge, the experts, the technical consultants and knows what time lunch is served. Makes you sick, doesn't it.

The Ellivators try to understand Micke's accent.

I sit in a corner reading through the notes. It's just like being back at school when you haven't done your homework, which happened to me rather regularly; so I'm quite proficient at getting up to speed in a limited timeframe. When I first speak with the judge for the snowmobile challenge, Jerry Bassett, I'm on top of my subject. Jerry is a very laid-back gentleman from St Paul, Minnesota, whose father ran one of the very early snowmobile dealerships back in the early sixties. Jerry has lived around snowmobiles more or less all his life. He's also lived through some very severe Minnesota winters, with snow six feet deep on the ground and the temperature so far below freezing it's best not to ask.

Actually, he's listening to Radio 4.

Jerry takes me through the history of the engineering. Although there are examples from the early part of the twentieth century, when motor vehicles were fitted with tracks and skis, the technology didn't really develop until the fifties. And appropriately enough, those early examples were constructed with exactly the same methods that the teams are using now. They raided scrapyards and used old motorbike engines, the chrome bumpers off cars for skis and whatever they could find to propel them.

The modern snowmobile that we see today is a very much more sophisticated machine that uses a lot of clever stuff, like lightweight two-stroke engines and amazingly moulded rubber and steel drive belts. These are really just like big loops of rubber matting with nobbles on, mounted on drive wheels like a tank track, that can spin around very fast. The idea is that they sit on top of the snow instead of sinking into it like a wheel, and hence are able to zoom these crazy things along as fast as powerful motorbikes zoom along the road.

As the build areas start to fill up with stuff, I begin to realize that the teams are in for a long and complicated day. This is not easier than monster trucks. In fact, as I sit on the throne watching the designs begin to take shape, I start to think it's a lot harder.

Backstage, I meet Chris Fiori, a very sporty looking man who is a big cheese in snowmobiling. He'll be teaching Cathy and I to ride one of these things when we go up into the mountains to test whatever the teams have built. He's worked on a load of movies that feature this type of technology, and because of this is a member of the Screen Actors Guild (SAG). That doesn't have to mean anything, except that the members of the guild are building up for a big strike and there have been doubts in the previous weeks as to whether Chris can get involved. It's been a touchy situation, because although RDF Media is a British company and the show we are making is for Channel 4 in England, it is also shown in the US on The Learning Channel. No one knows if the strike is going to affect the production of *Scrapheap Challenge* or its sister show *Junkyard Wars*, but understandably Chris doesn't want to be a strike-breaker. Before he started working with us, he had to check with SAG's lawyers; but he discovered that there really isn't a problem.

After the initial rush of scavenging, a classic picture starts to emerge. The Ellivators are piling up a massive array of scrap – motorbikes, tubing for building the framework, and for some reason a very large washing machine. They have a trail bike with a two-stroke engine, which judge Jerry thinks is the best bit of kit he's seen. I also know, courtesy of Tristan, Todd and John from the engineering department, that this bike is the only one on the yard. It's ideal because it's light; and lightness is everything, as I keep hearing from judge Jerry and both team experts. As usual, what they say and what they do don't always meld together, and eventually the Clan, as we are now calling them, drag in one of the biggest and most battered-looking motorbikes I've ever seen from the heap. It's a 1000cc Kawasaki with no front wheel. There are a lot of bits missing, but the Clan lads are all keen bikers and are pretty sure they can get it going.

For someone like me, remembering a lot of new names for each show is hard enough, but this week is particularly trying because the name Ellis is, by some quirk of fate, in very common usage. The McKarnow Clan are made up of father David Ellis and son Stephen Ellis, with Stephen's mate Colin Cleary. Over the other side of the wall, the Ellivators are made up of Ellis (Elli, get it?) Bergman and team members Roger Turner and Salih Ali. However, learning six names is nowhere near as hard as turning a very heavy bike into a lightweight, manoeuvrable snowmobile in ten hours, and already they only have nine left.

The weather gets steadily worse, the rain gets heavier and heavier, all the cameras have their little coats on, and Cathy and I climb into our amazingly warm all-weather parkas that we've only ever worn on test days on exposed coasts in

England. The backstage crew starts to manoeuvre the 'easy-ups' into position. These are collapsible covers held up by six lightweight aluminium supports, theoretically very simple to erect if you have enough people on hand. Of course, they've done time on *Scrapheap* for a few years now. As a result, they are in a terminal state – legs missing, broken support struts held together with soggy tape and big rips in the once-waterproof fabric. Still, putting them up is better than leaving the teams to suffer in the elements, and we all shuffle and shout as we get them into position. Everyone lends a hand and for someone whose job is merely to watch and comment, this is one of the few occasions where I can actually do something useful.

By lunchtime, the rain has eased off a little, but it's still cold and overcast. The teams have also eased off a little. The Clan are feeling very confident. They've got their bike engine running and it's sounding good. They are still looking for enough wheels to use in the conveyor belt propulsion system, though. And the actual belting material itself. And some drive chains, drive sprockets, steel to construct a frame and some sort of ski for the front end. Other than that, they're doing really well.

The Ellivators have decided to ditch their initial plan for a conveyor belt affair. They have opted to use the drum from inside the washing machine as a kind of giant rear wheel. They plan to build two independent skis, mounted on what were once the front forks of the bike, which will let them steer and give them stability. The obvious thing about this design is that what it may lack in the large belt drive business, it gains in the lightweight department. It looks light, and the increasingly large pile of steel building up in the McKarnow Clan area looks very sink-deep-in-the-snow heavy.

A washing machine drum, of course. Isn't that what Micke asked for?

Director Amanda, who sounds like she should be leading the Berkshire hunt but is totally into the detail of the build, asks me to go in and talk to the Clan about the weight and drive belt issues. It's a standard procedure; the experts outside the build area are conferring with each other. Chris Fiury and judge Jerry both think the Clan's machine is going to be too heavy – they are effectively going to build a giant and clearly very powerful snow digger. They think the only direction the machine will go is down, into the snow. Once Amanda and Jeremy have heard this, either Cathy or I have to go into the build area and talk to the teams to introduce these worries early on, in the hope that they get the message and change their design. It's a fatally flawed system, as the teams almost invariably explain to me that I am hopelessly wrong and they have it all worked out. The Clan are no exception, and Stephen Ellis, the team captain, makes it clear that they believe their engine is powerful enough to rocket them along at a fairly breakneck speed. He doesn't use the term breakneck, but that's what it looks like he means, because the one bit they have now constructed is the front end and the 'steering'. This is basically a truck's bumper, fitted on to a thick steel pole, which is in turn attached to the two front forks that once held the motorbike wheel. It looks very high and therefore a little unstable… no, I'm being kind. This machine, even without its drive mechanism, looks psychotically unstable. It looks like it needs a coat with very long sleeves that fasten at the back. The Clan team members have a go at me while I am with them, because apparently I once used the term 'the best our English boffins can come up with' in a 'Best of *Scrapheap Challenge*' video. They pick me up on my Southern, exclusive, ignore-the-rest-of-the-country snobbism. I should have said 'British boffins', of course. I always get very confused over these issues even though I have a Welsh name, I'm effectively as Welsh as cappuccino. I always put 'English' when I answer the nationality section on passport forms and visa

The reassuring *Scrapheap* sound of grinding metal.

applications. I don't say 'British' on purpose, because I think it's unfair on all the other countries that the term includes: Scotland, Wales and Northern Ireland. I find it hard to believe I said 'English boffins', if only because it doesn't sound as good as 'British Boffins', but I have to accept that they are right...

I like the Clan because they are the only team to have ever seen any of my plays and shows at the Edinburgh festival. They must be

Cath, what's going on? Do you know?

some of the very few locals who actually go and see some of the thousands of performances that are on each day during the festivities. They also know all about Ms Cheese and Mr Hamm, which are mine and Cathy's alter egos on the show. During the second series we had a wonderful camera operator called Steen Ericsson from Sweden, and he inspired these probably fundamentallyun-politically correct characters. Mr Hamm and Ms Cheese are basically two Euro-reporters who speak in a strange, lilting, Scandinavian way. I would say something like, 'Welcome to the scrap of the heap, enjoying very much the build we are doing, and now over to Ms Cheese.'

And Cathy, who always claims she is not a performer but who can turn in a mean – and, I'm sure, equally deeply offensive to Swedish people – impersonation of Swedish TV 'lady' Ms Cheese, would reply, 'Thank you Mr Hammy Hamm, I am Helga Cheese and this is my heap.'

It was all pointless, stupid off-camera stuff that somehow managed to appear on film, and was then used as a bit of light relief on the *Scrapheap* video. I don't even remember it properly, but the Clan do. I only hope that Micke, the Swedish expert on the Ellivators team, hasn't heard about it. He does have the same lilting accent, but he doesn't say much, so we're not tempted to impersonate him.

Cathy and I do a little chat (not as Hamm and Cheese) around the back of the set. We huddle close because of the wind and have a laugh at the teams' expense. I always feel mean doing this because I know they are working incredibly hard against ludicrous odds, but somehow it seems to work. There is an endless fascination with watching how teams work and seeing how they solve the myriad problems they are faced with. Clearly, if you aren't directly involved with making something and you stand and watch, you get an overview and can see things that the teams can't. But it's such an unfair advantage. I've always known that if I was in a team, especially as a captain, I would make such a mess, forget so many vital components and delegate tasks so badly we would need ten weeks to make a plate rack.

AS THE PANIC CONTINUES

By late afternoon, the rain is coming down in buckets. Judge Jerry and I sit on a very wet throne in our very wet clothes and discuss the tasks the teams still have ahead. It seems to be mainly drive systems for the Clan, which even at this late stage haven't really taken shape, and steering systems for the Ellivators, of which there is no sign in any way, not even potential components.

As night falls and everyone is now cold and wet, a dull panic has set in off-stage. Jeremy is very worried that neither team is going to finish within anything near the ten-hour limit. He is hoping, based on previous experience, that somehow the teams will be galvanized into making that bit of extra effort and that they'll really make something happen in the remaining two hours.

I announce the two-hour call a little early – *Scrapheap* time is very elastic – and neither team seems to complain that the last time check was only fifty minutes ago. It does the trick. Suddenly, there's a flurry of activity, and piles of loose components that are indistinguishable from general lumps of scrap on the floor are suddenly joined together. Within half an hour there is a recognizable drive system appearing on the Clan's Flying Scotsman machine, and a complex double ski suspension system taking shape on the Ellivators' side of the build. The last two hours are spent keeping the cameras, tools and equipment as dry as we can. I end up sweeping a puddle of water away from the electric welder in the Ellivators' build area because – call me picky – when I see an electrical cable and extension plug lying in a puddle, I get very tense.

As the panic continues, we get reports from Mammoth (the place where we are doing the test) that they have just had six inches of fresh snow, which means that conditions could be very powdery and soft. This is a worry for both teams, as soft snow is harder to travel over than hard, packed stuff.

By the time I tell the teams to finish, they have done us proud – once again. Lying in damp build areas are two machines that pretty much impersonate snowmobiles. The Ellivators' machine looks very smart, lightweight and almost ready to hit the piste. The rear washing machine drum drive mechanism is very impressive. They have built a new rear end on the bike and extended the drive sprocket mounting from the motorbike engine to enable the chain to run to a bigger drive sprocket on the drum. They have also welded a series of 'paddles' on to the drum, lengths of L-section steel that should dig into the snow and give them traction.

Over the wall, the Clan have finally mounted their enormous, heavy-looking belt-drive system on to their enormous, heavy motorbike with its enormous, heavy front-mounted ski. The bike they are using is a shaft drive design – it doesn't have a chain, so they have had to weld on a chain sprocket to what was once the rear wheel mounting. A chain runs from this down on to another sprocket, which is in turn attached to the wheels that will turn the belt. It's all very *Scrapheap* and very prone to classic wibbly-wobbliness. They don't seem concerned about this at all; they are very happy with this top-heavy monster.

Both teams cheer wildly when I announce that their time is up. It never ceases to amaze me how much energy they have – after charging around all day in the rain, building insane machines that have very little chance of working, they all seem wildly happy and fulfilled.

There is a scene of total chaos backstage as we start to clear up and change. Tara, the never-tiring production co-ordinator, is running around giving everyone soggy call sheets for

We could be looking at speeds of up to 60mph. Or, er, zero.

the test day. The teams are drinking beer in the little shed that serves as our 'green room' and production office. Eloise is busy handing out snow boots for everyone to try on. The organization behind this challenge is greater than ever. We are going to be testing these machines above the snowline and it's mid-April. The snowline is very high up, over 9,000 feet, so it's going to be bitterly cold. Amid the chaos, the wet, the cold and the puddles I try on a pair of enormous snow boots and find to my surprise that they fit. They are duly tagged and thrown into an enormous pile in the corner. Everywhere I look there are clothes, shoes, helmets and bits of camera equipment. Jeremy Cross is looking exhausted, he's had a day of it; in fact, I suspect he's having a year of it, as the *Scrap* pandemonium never stops. There are always 4,000 new problems to solve each day, and although he clearly loves the challenge, I don't envy him one bit.

Somehow, sense finally emerges from the chaos as the teams climb back into the bus and head back to their hotel. Spud is still running around with cameras, Greg is pulling down all the radio antennas used for the sound equipment; everything is soaked, dirty, or damp, or all three.

I get to bed at about 12.30am, knowing that the following day is definitely going to be a tough one.

The Test

Directly opposite the RDF Media production office on Ventura Boulevard is a drug store car park, and in this, a chrome-trimmed bus – very similar to the one in the movie *Speed* – is parked, surrounded by piles of bags, boxes of equipment and stacks of bottled water.

Mammoth is around 300 miles north, in the High Sierras mountain range. We are due to leave at 10.00am but of course, there are complications. It wouldn't be right if there weren't, so we end up standing around in the hot morning sun with the teams, considering the irony of the weather. It's a hot, dazzlingly bright Californian day, as different to the build day as it could be. Los Angeles really doesn't look good in the rain; it needs sun to work, to make the palm trees look at home and to get that heat blast from the acres of concrete.

We pile on to the bus and are counted off like schoolchildren by Tara. The bus driver has forgotten his log book, which by law he has to carry when driving, so our first stop is 20 miles up the freeway, where his mother is waiting for him. We pull up on a freeway ramp and there she is, standing by her pick-up truck, log book in hand.

That's about as exciting as it gets. We have a five-hour journey ahead of us and the bus, it has to be said, isn't the most comfortable thing I have ever travelled in.

'When did they get this thing out of retirement?' asks Jacob, one of the American camera operators. Jacob is a tall, long-haired dude who has become a favourite with myself and Cathy – he's always smiling, he never complains and he seems to love the show. All the American crew have remarked at one time or another that they really enjoy working on it. They seem to appreciate the very informal atmosphere that prevails. Clearly, American productions are very much more hierarchical; certain people don't speak to, or mix with, other people. The 'talent', which believe it or not refers to me, are usually protected from the rest of the crew and cosseted beyond belief. The Americans seem very impressed that Cathy and I will muck in with everyone so readily, but it seems normal to us.

The bus drones on through small roadside towns as it heads north. It's only after a few hours that I can see we are slowly climbing. After about three hours we start to spot snow-covered peaks, and we start to wind up some steeper hills. After four hours, we're surrounded by them, and pull over for a break in a sun-drenched rest area. Everyone runs for the toilets as, although there is a 'washroom' at the back of the bus, it's not too pleasant. An impromptu game of frisbee starts up in the car park, and while I'm failing to catch or throw with any great skill, a woman comes up to me and asks if I am in a show called *Junkyard Wars*. She is a student from Santa Barbara who has just been on a field trip in Yosemite National Park, but she and all her mates watch the show avidly. She is thrilled to hear that there are to be more episodes and that we are recording them in America. I look around at our location. We are in an area of vast, open desert; there are very few houses, let alone towns, for miles in any direction; two

'I hope that 'S' doeshn't shtand for Shmersh, Mishter Goldfinger...'

other camper vans are the only other signs of human life. I never get recognized in Los Angeles when I cruise around in my shades looking really cool. Yet here, in the middle of nowhere, when I've just dropped an easy frisbee catch and the crew are telling me what a tosser I am, I am spotted by a fan of the show.

Five hours after leaving Ventura Boulevard, the bus pulls up in front of the reception of the Juniper Springs Lodge. I had heard the name and had a vision of a small, Alpine-like wooden building with a pointy, snow-covered roof. It is, of course, a massive hotel. It is built of wood, but we're talking huge great spars of redwood, just too big to have come from anything we would recognize as a tree. After the long drive, it's a fantastic place to arrive at. Within minutes of getting off the bus, I am swimming in a hot outdoor pool at the rear of the hotel, with snow all around and huge snow-covered peaks making an incredibly dramatic backdrop.

One by one the teams and crew arrive and we take over the pool and the surrounding hot tubs. Director Amanda, Cathy, assistant producer Helen, Eloise and I sit in a hot tub and drink vodka. Well, they drink vodka, I have a sip and feel like I'm about to pass out. The air is thinner here; I've never experienced it before. You only have to climb a flight of stairs and you feel yourself gasping for breath – your heart starts beating wildly and you start to worry about how out of condition you are.

'You've really got to drink a lot of water, it's very dehydrating,' says Amanda as she takes another swig of vodka. Yeah, right.

We have a big production and safety meeting in a huge inflated white bubble of a building close to the hotel. It's pretty much the end of the skiing season, and although there are still a few hardy snowboarders and their ilk in evidence, the place is pretty quiet.

We go through the following day's events, hear the mandatory safety briefing from Peter Clews, receive more warnings about sunburn, dehydration and what to do if we start to suffer from altitude sickness. We are also warned not to wander around the streets after dark as there are a lot of grizzly bears that come into the small community and raid the rubbish bins.

A meal has been provided by the hotel, and I hear stories from Clint, who, being a South African beach dude, has never had much contact with snow. He arrived the day before to help set up the challenge course, but he's had time to try a bit of snowboarding and it's obvious he really loves it.

'I came down this really steep hill and fell over at about 30mph, it was fantastic.' He is beaming and a different colour from when I last saw him. 'The sun is really intense, man, and you get sunburnt under your chin 'cos of the reflection. It's amazing.'

As I walk back to the hotel with Jeremy, I keep a close lookout for marauding grizzly bears, but I don't see any. I have a 5.30am wake-up call booked for the morning, so I don't fancy joining the teams and crew on their Mammoth pub crawl. As there is only one pub in Mammoth, I assume it won't take them that long.

At 6.00am, I've spent half an hour getting strapped into all my snow gear. My boots, specially designed for use on a snowboard, are incredibly warm and comfy, except that they push your legs forward in that weird snowboarding way so you can't really stand up without bending them. I stumble out into the startlingly cold, clear air and make my way to our breakfast rendezvous. A quick bite to eat, then we're off up the mountain in a Jeep, along a winding road surrounded on both sides by huge piles of snow. We stop in a car park and a weird orange thing rumbles towards us through the woods. It's a sort of snow bus, a machine with enormously wide tank tracks and a snow plough on the front, with seating for eight people in the back. We cram the camera and sound

'Really, James.'

equipment inside and clamber aboard. The sun is up now and everything is dazzlingly bright. Up this high (I don't know exactly how high it is, but it's very high) there is deep snow everywhere. The driver, a New Zealander who's lived in the area for years, tells us he has skied on Mammoth Mountain in July. Up this high, the snow never melts.

I COULD FEEL LIKE A REALLY OLD BLOKE WHO'S PAST IT

We start to climb up an impossibly steep slope, but the snow bus has no trouble. However, on the slippery sideways-facing seats in the passenger compartment, the two people sitting at the rear are soon suffering a severe squashing. The whole bus is at about a 30-degree angle and there is nothing we can do to stop sliding back. We are all holding cameras or bags or slabs of water bottles, and huge caterpillar tracks don't exactly make for a smooth ride. When we finally reach the location, I am really feeling the difference that this altitude makes to a body. Just climbing down out of the snow bus and walking ten feet up the hill makes me feel like I've been running for an hour. I could feel like a really old bloke who's past it, but it's obvious everyone else is in the same boat.

When we are ready to shoot, I take off my dark glasses and I can't see a thing because the light is incredible. I'm sure people who have been skiing will be very familiar with all this. However, for a first-timer like me, it's all very new and quite painful in the eye department.

When I have done my first pieces to camera, I hear a distant motorbike engine. It grows louder until, suddenly, over a bluff behind me, a snowmobile flies into the air. It's coming towards us, up a hill that it would be very difficult to stand on, let alone walk up, and it's going as fast as a motorbike would along a flat street. It screams past us and heads even further up the hill, then the rider seems to throw it into the air over a soft pile of snow. It turns and comes to a halt right next to the snow bus without any trouble whatsoever. I hear myself thinking in American: 'Hey dude, these things are cool.'

We then shoot a James Bond-type sequence, where I chase a baddie skier down the hill at incredible speed. Of course, I do all my own stunts, and anyone who says otherwise is a total liar.

When the very brave snowmobile rider has finished doing my stunt for me, we trundle off down the mountain again. This time the person at the front – me – gets squashed by four people and half a ton of equipment, but I quite like it.

When we are back down to a part of the mountain that is only very high up, as opposed to too high up to breathe, Cathy and I do another little set-piece opener where she is the Moneypenny to my Bond. I, of course, can only do an impression of Chris Barrie doing an impression of Sean Connery.

Robert: Mish Moneypenny will fill you in.

Cathy: Really, James! Oh, very well then…

This time I actually do ride the snowmobile, having had only a ten-second go before the cameras roll. I'm not saying they are dead easy to drive, but there's basically a lever that makes you go faster, another one that stops you, and handle bars to steer with. You'd have to be pretty stupid to crash the damn thing.

As Cathy and I pull ourselves out of a very deep snow drift that I have crashed into, turning the very stable, safe snowmobile on to its side, Cathy reminds me of this. She is then whooshed off to interview the teams who, from what I've heard over the intermittently working walkie-talkies, are having what can only be described as another 'major tinker' with their machines. Apparently, the Clan's machine is working rather well and they are very excited, but the Ellis are still struggling to get their front suspension to do anything other than squash down.

I then have the best fun I have had on *Scrappers* for a long time. I get to ride a snowmobile through the beautiful woodlands of Mammoth Mountain while

A camera operator films Robert coming down the slope: 'Go faster, he hasn't got a clue how to drive it!'

a cameraman on another snowmobile films me. Yes, this time I am actually doing my own stunts, although I just ride along quite safe snow tracks. These things are really powerful. They don't feel it at first, as you have to open the throttle quite a bit to get them going, but once they move – oh, my Lord, they really shift. I also discover they kick up quite a bit of snow; as I ride behind the cameraman, who is bravely sitting backwards on a bumping snowmobile filming me, I get a constant fresh faceful of snow powder. Very refreshing at 9,000 feet.

We finally descend to where the scrap snowmobile race is going to take place. We eat a speedy lunch on the hoof – we have to get this in the can before 4.00pm because we all have to ride back to Los Angeles in the bus the same night. The teams fly home tomorrow, crossing paths with the new teams who are just arriving for the next challenge.

Now, you might think that there are two kinds of competition: the sporting kind, like a race or a footie match where individuals or teams compete against each other and one wins, end of story; and the sort of competition where you have to use your wits, like *Who Wants To Be a Millionaire?*, where you have to be clever and quick and then someone wins and that's it, end of story.

Clearly influenced by sophisticated Scandinavian design...

But there is a different kind of competition. A totally mad *Scrapheap Challenge,* one that has no pre-set rules, no precedent because every competition is completely different, and one where the winners are quite often really depressed because it means they have to go through the whole back-breaking nightmare again.

While we are standing on the hard-packed snow of the *Scrapheap Challenge* snowmobile race circuit, we are discovering that even within the all-encompassing madhouse rules of the *Heap,* there is yet another sub-genre: 'The snowmobile-that-only-moves-one-foot-and-then-falls-to-bits race'.

This is how Round One pans out when the McKarnow Clan drag their huge heavyweight beast onto the track. They are a good fifty feet from the start line to give both teams the chance of getting off to a flying start; the Clan know that once they get going, their machine will just roar around the circuit. Judge Jerry is only going to time them from the moment they pass under the *Scrapheap* starting flag that Clint has rigged

... in comparison to the Scottish aesthetic we see here.

up. The engine starts first time. Always a bad sign. Then, bang! Bits of metal fly everywhere, the team run around shouting, the engine dies. They have actually moved, well, I say a foot, but I'm being kind... probably the mere vibration of the engine shuddered them down the slope a little.

Both machines are being ridden by their experts, Dave Patterson on the Clan's machine and Micke Nordstrum on the Ellis'. This is due to our various safety meetings, where it was decided that as the machines had the potential to travel at very high speed over hard-packed snow, it was just too dangerous to let the inexperienced teams take the controls. I don't want to say 'Yeah, right,' but it's very tempting. Oh, OK then, I will. 'Yeah, right.'

As the afternoon wears on, this ruling is becoming more and more comical. Next up, the Ellis' bring their super-lightweight machine on to the track. It looks good, it looks very good, even some of the bemused skiers who are waiting to go on a chair lift to one side of the track are looking on, intrigued. Maybe this is the future of snowmobiles – maybe in years to come there will be international Grand Prix races with this type of machine: a motorbike with a washing machine drum

Cathy checks out team morale before the 'off'.

traction unit. I can believe it – that is, until Micke starts the baby up and puts it into gear. It does move, the little paddle blades on the big drum are digging into the snow and pushing the machine along. Aha, we have a functioning scrap snowmobile. At the present rate, the Ellis' are going to win hands down. This thing is going like a dream.

'I knew it would work!' shouts judge Jerry, and it is indeed a great sight. It always is, after seeing the effort and sweat that has gone into producing this thing. When they actually do something they are supposed to, it's a fantastic moment, especially for the teams. The Ellis' are triumphant, jumping in the air and whooping… until a big lump of dirty metal falls on to the pristine snow and the Ellis' snowmobile slumps to a halt.

'It is very broken,' says Micke, which is the first thing I've heard him say all day. It seems, after a very quick inspection, that the weld that held the sprocket extension out on a steel arm from the original drive has, not really very surprisingly, snapped clean off. Without hesitation the team rush for the mobile welder – a little generator and welding kit that is always on hand for the teams when they need to do a little tinker; or, in today's case, a major tinker.

While the Ellivators are busy re-welding the broken drive shaft, the McKarnow Clan have managed to repair their monster snow machine for another run. Again, the engine starts first time. There'd been doubts about this happening because engines have a problem running at this altitude – the lack of oxygen makes it harder to get a spark and therefore ignite the fuel.

The Clan push like crazy and, yes, the machine starts to run under its own power. Dave Patterson is sitting on top of the crazy looking thing and he is steering. All the predictions that the steering wouldn't work are wrong, and it is moving, the belt is giving them really good traction, it isn't sinking into the snow, it's really working. The Clan cheer as a motorbike-powered snowmobile, exactly what we asked them to make, passes the start line and makes its precarious way up the gentle slope of the circuit. We all cheer too soon, of course; suddenly there's a noise we are all going to hear a great deal in the coming stages of the increasingly stop-start contest. The engine's powered roar suddenly changes to an out-of-control scream. The drive chain has come off and the Clan's Flying Scotsman stops in its tracks, or maybe I should say on its tracks. It's going nowhere – fast, slow or otherwise.

There is a hasty production meeting in the snow. We have faced this kind of mid-competition crisis before, but it always seems more catastrophic at the time. We are really not having anything that can be classified as a race. We are merely watching two teams fix hopelessly fragile machines in the middle of a snowfield. Jeremy decides on drastic action. We will have to measure how far the teams get past the starting line with only three restarts. That is, if the machine breaks down or comes to a halt for whatever reason, they can only fix and restart it three times each. We are pushing our time limit as it is; we have to be clear and in the bus in less than an hour. As *Scrapheap* crises go, and we usually have a couple each episode, this is turning out to be a biggie.

Jeremy and judge Jerry put this idea to the teams and everyone agrees that this is the only way forward. I am furnished with a tape measure and we take the first measurement from the start line to the Clan's stationary machine. They have managed forty feet.

They put their chain back on, the machine starts running again and with a push, it crawls up the hill. It gets another fifty feet this time before the chain again slips its moorings and flies around like an angry horse's tail. The

The Ellivators add a bit of man-power to the horsepower.

Clan lads dash up the track, followed by everyone it seems; all semblance of a circuit, or any form of directorial control, in fact any form of basic TV sense has long since left us. We are in pure scrapland, flying by the seat of our collective pants, trying all the time to allow good camera shots but letting events dictate themselves. On the Clan's third and final attempt they actually climb up the slope of snow quite effectively, gaining at least another sixty or so feet before their problem chain throws its third and final wobbly. We complete our measurements and, along with Cathy,

Just to prove...

agree that in ten minutes, three seconds the Clan have covered 160 feet of snow. Cathy works out that their average speed over this distance was around a quarter of a mile an hour, thus rocketing the machine into the *Scrapheap* hall of fame as the slowest vehicle ever produced out of rubbish. Not bad.

The Ellis' are up next with their reinforced drive shaft. Micke starts up the engine and with a hearty push from the team, their snowmobile starts to power its way towards the start line.

'It's looking good,' says judge Jerry, as Micke struggles with the controls. The washing machine wheel is spinning away like mad, throwing lumps of snow high into the air. There is no disputing the fact that this machine works, it goes faster, it looks more stable; it's maybe not as funny-looking, but as we watch Micke power past the start line, it seems to everyone that the Ellis' have it in the bag. Then, ping, the engine screams, Micke stops, the machine stops, everything stops. Something has gone horribly wrong. They have covered maybe seventy feet, very fast. The Clan are looking worried.

... that both machines could move under their own power. A bit.

The rest of the Ellivators team rush to assist. They are all over the bike in seconds trying to work out what's gone wrong. The clock is ticking. By the time the bike starts again, they've used up five minutes. It seems that nothing has gone wrong with their build; it's the gearbox on the bike – the extra strain from the washing machine drum drive is causing it to kick out of gear. This time Micke is going for broke. They've had one restart. He sends a shower of snow into the air but doesn't move; the washing machine drum is merely digging a big hole in the snow. The team push and shove and eventually it starts moving again, this time for a mere ten feet before the tell-tale scream of the engine tells us something has gone wrong again.

There is a manic inspection of the drive mechanism. Something has broken, but the team decide they can live with it. With a push and a shove, they get started again and head up the hill, towards the point that the Clan managed to reach. It is anyone's guess as to whether the Ellivators will break the half-mile an hour speed record set by their opponents. It shouldn't be such a tall order; but this is *Scrapheap Challenge*, after all... and anything can happen.

Seven hours later...

The teams have been dropped off at their hotel, we said farewell to the losers, and see you again to the winners. Everyone seems happy, the crew are exhausted, and I have managed to sleep from Mammoth Mountain to Mojave, which is about 250 miles. My rear end is totally numb, and when we get out of the bus, the air is warm. We have to unload a mass of equipment from the belly of the bus, but somehow the team spirit that makes this job such a good one comes to the fore. Everyone moans, everyone helps, I start carrying great coils of heavy electrical cable into the production offices, only to be told by Zak, our ever-present, ever-patient driver that it's in the wrong place and should be in his van.

At 1.00am I go to bed, worried that I won't be able to sleep because I slept for so long on the bus. Next thing I know, it's another hot, bright LA morning.

WHITEWATER RIDER

That clear blue sky, a huge dazzling canopy, can only mean one thing when it's still 5.30am – it's going to be a hottie. The streets around the yard are dusty and fairly pungent by the time I arrive. I have only recently discovered that one of California's biggest landfill sights is only a few hundred yards away, though it's easy to spot, because huge flocks of sea birds circle around above it. When I stand on top of the scrap observation tower I can see the rows of garbage trucks winding their way up the side of a medium-sized and ever-growing man-made mountain.

As usual, the teams are already togged up and standing around talking excitedly. There's a very good atmosphere on the site, for a number of reasons. The sky is clear and the light is beautiful, which cheers us up even if we are breathing fairly toxic fumes all the time. And this programme is the last of the heats. After this challenge, we will have recorded six shows and will have met all the teams who are taking part in this year's series. It's been a pretty tough schedule, and everyone is having a break after this recording. I am off home via Sydney, where I will pick up my kids, who I've missed something rotten; Cathy's sister is visiting and they are going off on jaunts together. Jeremy Cross is off on a little holiday with his family, while camera operator Andy Calvert is going back home. All the American crew seem to be off somewhere, or moving on to other jobs.

Robert: That's a team over there.
Cathy: Well done, you're catching on at last.

'Hey, how are you?' I get asked repeatedly by charming, smiling Americans. The crew has really clicked together now; we have learned how to talk to each other.

'I'm good,' I say. 'How are you?'

'I'm good too.'

That's what you're meant to say. I had to ask. I would usually say 'Hello' when someone asked me how I was, and it always felt a little awkward, like I hadn't answered their question.

We have all learned little phrases from each other. The previous week, Todd, the amiable giant from the engineering department (or 'the lovely Todd' as he is now known) said without prompting, 'There's a bloke at the gate with a load of equipment.' They now refer to a man they don't know as a 'bloke' or a 'geezer', and we say garbage, not rubbish; trunk, not boot; hood, not bonnet, and a myriad other slightly different terms.

Another hot day on the set. Ideal for running around building things.

Anyway, I meet the teams. This week they're the Body Snatchers, three paramedics from Milton Keynes, and the Xtinguishers, three firefighters from Kent. They are a very friendly and talkative bunch, which Cathy and I take as a good sign.

We go through the usual rigmarole of a delayed start, but by 9.15am, the teams are on their way to building something I cannot yet conceive of.

'Body Snatchers, Xtinguishers, your task in the next ten hours is to build a craft that will take to the rapids – a scraptastic whitewater rider.'

The teams are thrilled. They run fast, they laugh, they talk, they are totally up for it. By the time they are standing around the board listening to their experts, the sun is already very warm.

With the Xtinguishers is Alan Pickard, a jet bike designer and world speed record holder for personal watercraft. Alan is from Yorkshire, and he won his speed record on a jet ski on Lake Windermere in October 2000. He clearly knows all there is to know about jet skis and how they move fast. What he is suggesting to his team is that they construct a flat-bottomed boat built out of the roof of a vehicle, something like a Transit van, which they will cut off and turn upside down. He then wants them to find the drive system from a jet ski or similar to provide the power. The idea seems to be that they build a boat that 'planes', which means it goes fast enough to lift itself up and skim over the surface of the water. Sounds good, and highly unlikely, from my hard-won experience. Things that are powerful enough to fly along the surface of water are really carefully built over months, tested, and redesigned using specially manufactured parts that cost loads of money. They are not thrown together in ten hours using the roof of an old van and some half-bust-up bits of a cracked jet ski.

Over on the other side of the wall, the Body Snatchers are listening to their expert come up with an even more unlikely idea. Boat-builder Colin Poole wants to build an airboat, a huge metal pontoon with an enormous engine mounted on a stand at the rear. This is in turn connected to an aeroplane propeller that will spin very fast and drive their boat along 'like a rocket'.

As he speaks, Colin reveals that he has already built an airboat, which he tested on his lake in Southport. He tells the team the story and they listen intently, their faces a picture of delight. The engine and propeller made so much noise when he started them up that he had to abandon the project as too disturbing for the neighbours. That wasn't just the people who lived right next to the lake; the airboat could be heard five miles away.

'Brilliant,' says Gerry Lea, one of the scavengers. It's the perfect reaction for this show; for some reason that eludes me, we all love really noisy machines that upset people five miles away.

'Come on then, let's get cracking,' says Tim Miles, their gentle-looking team captain. Gerry and Debbie Bilton jump into the six-wheeler and they're off. Yes, I did say Debbie Bilton and yes, she is the first, and indeed only, woman in this year's season. Debbie is a paramedic who works with Tim and Gerry, driving ambulances to emergencies all around the Milton Keynes area. She is very keen to take part and seems undaunted by the task ahead.

Body Snatcher Debbie pulls her weight.

'There's a woman team member!' I say to Cathy. 'An actual woman.'

'I know, I know, I'm so excited!' Cathy squeals. It has been her driving ambition for four years to get women to compete in the show, a driving ambition that has garnered results. Who could forget Anne and Kali from Series One, or Babs Munsen from Series Two, or Diana, the seventy-two year-old demon scavenger from the Mothers of Invention in Series Three?

Who, indeed, could forget her immortal line when the Mothers were finally beaten in the bridge-building challenge?

'Beats making bloody jam!'

Xtinguisher Westy adopts the position.

But it seems increasingly hard to find women who are prepared to have a go, which is a shame. There is no reason on earth why *Scrapheap* should be an exclusively 'lads' show, and although I am very proud of the lads who have appeared, a few more women engineers would be great. Go on, don't just sit there, get an all-women team together and apply. Believe me, you've got a pretty good chance of getting on.

I go into the Body Snatchers' build area to talk to team captain Tim and expert Colin about what they are going to attempt. Colin wants lots of barrels – not those round steel oil barrels that have been fairly ubiquitous on previous challenges – but big, sealed steel boxes, like bulk storage containers, because he is, I am glad to hear, worried about having a high centre of gravity. I am worried about that too, but I am also worried that the whole thing will sit in the middle of the river and go around in circles. My fears are well-grounded, because I saw this happen when a team made up entirely of Royal Navy personnel built an amphibious vehicle which did exactly that. Colin assures me it won't happen. He plans to build two huge air rudders right behind the fan that will steer the boat and keep it going in the direction they want it to.

I ask Tim if he's made anything like this in the past. He hasn't, but there's no doubting his credentials when it comes to fixing stuff up and working out how to solve problems with minimal materials. After leaving the Army in 1993, Tim went to Albania where he rebuilt schools and village hospitals, renovated medical equipment and taught the local people about basic healthcare. Building a whitewater rider should be a doddle for this geezer.

I have a quick chat with Debbie Bilton about the opposition. I have heard rumours backstage that there is a bit of rivalry between paramedics and firefighters.

'They just love to cut the roof off anything,' she says matter-of-factly. 'If we get to the scene of a crash and there's a roof on a car, they'll cut it off. Doesn't matter if there's no one in the car, they'll still cut it off. We call them roof-cutters, or sometimes drip stands.'

'Drip stands?'

BODY SNATCHERS ARE GOING FOR BIG. I LIKE BIG.

'Yes, when we're treating a patient at an accident, we might have to insert an intravenous drip, and we need someone to hold the bag. Firemen are good at that, they like to stand around and hold things, if they're not cutting a roof off. Or we call them Trumpton.'

I had no idea there could be such rivalry between these two arms of the emergency services. I think of them working together as a well-oiled machine, not sniping away at each other as they step over the debris on their way to save some poor soul trapped in a car wreck.

Cathy has been talking to the Xtinguishers, and we genuinely don't speak to each other before we meet on the throne for the first of our little chats. I learn about the horse box roof that the scavengers, Ian Fergusson (nickname Fergie) and Nigel Morley (nickname, er, Morley) have already cut off. They don't hang about, these firefighters, they've already cut a roof off and they've only been at it half an hour. They have also located an engine and a jet boat propeller. They are busy grinding and cutting and welding. Bish bosh, job done, by the looks of things. The Xtinguishers are following their expert's plan, which is a good sign: they're going for a flat-bottomed boat that will theoretically skim across the water rather than plough through it. As Cathy and I discuss the challenge, we see Debbie and Gerry returning with more and more enormous steel barrels on the Body Snatchers' side. There is already a noticeable size differential between the two teams. It's very clear that the Body Snatchers are going for big. I like big.

I have a quick break, during which I meet Steve Curtis, our judge for this challenge. He's a big rangey blonde dude who wears a wide-brimmed sun hat and looks the man least likely to be the off-shore world power boat race winner three times. Steve has driven boats (I say driven because I don't think you 'captain' one of these monsters) over big waves while travelling at over 100mph. He has also had a bash at whitewater racing, which, I learn, originated in New Zealand, where they have more than their share of white water. The professionals, if you can call someone who steers a power boat up a waterfall a professional, use aluminium boats with very powerful engines. As Steve and I sit on the throne and go through the various options, it's clear he's a judge who is going to be less than overwhelmed by the skill of the teams.

'They're both rubbish,' he says with cheeky charm. 'I think they'll both sink as soon as they hit the water.'

I get the sneaky suspicion he is not convinced that either will be up to the challenge. Not only have they got to float, they have to push their way upstream against the fast-flowing current of a rock-strewn river, and they have to be able to steer around the more deadly obstacles. As I look at each work area, I have to admit that Steve may have a point. When pressured to choose which team he thinks will win, he eventually decides to root for the Xtingiushers because their design, in theory at least, is tried and tested.

Off the set, I see Jeremy and Paul, the director on this challenge, sitting in a corner going over the programme we are now shooting. I quite often overhear Jeremy conversing about a show we are going to be doing in a month's time, or next week; his workload is unrelenting and he seems to relish it. They talk about the shape of the show, always the shape; they have to be thinking ahead – how they are going to cut the mountain of material they will end up with into something that will tell the story of the challenge in an engaging and education-ally informative way.

Steve: They're both rubbish!
Robert: Can he say that?

I know I couldn't do their job – I'd forget something vital – and I notice they spend a lot of time going through their shooting scripts, methodically ticking off the things they need to get done. It's all too easy to miss an essential aspect of the build; there's just so much to be sure of recording that the directors have to check their lists all the time. I am unaware of three-quarters of what's going on during filming. I just move when I'm told to move, and talk when I'm told to talk. If I did try to understand what was happening in all the various departments, I'd be wearing the jacket with the very long sleeves in minutes. I sit down next to Nat Grouille. He's on the phone, and as he talks I realize he's busy organizing another challenge, one we won't be doing until later in the year. That's when we start doing the semi-finals and final, and the grand final of finals, and then of course the super, international ultra-mega wars final of the absolute end of final finals.

But that is then; this is now, and in the Body Snatchers' build area, all is not well. Scavengers Debbie and Gerry can only find eight barrels. They are just the sort expert Colin wanted, sort of square, heavy-duty fellows, but there simply aren't enough of them. As I call the eight-hour time warning, their build area is littered with the large blue square barrels. They look very heavy, and the whole thing is looking enormous, as I watch, I see Gerry drive in with a small block Chevy engine in his trailer. We have been here long enough now that I can tell at a glance the difference between a big block and small block V8. The fact that it's called a small block doesn't have a great deal to do with its size; it's still a huge thing, and according to the drawing on the board it's going to be mounted very high on their boat. And according to every boating expert I have ever met on *Scrapheap*, and I've met a few, there seems to be a simple-to-follow design rule: 'Big heavy weight high up on small boat: very tippy-over-making. Big heavy weight high up on small boat that is actually a powerful engine with massive propeller attached to the rear, creating vast amounts of thrust and torque: totally tippy-over-making.' It's all looking very scary.

'It's not like a flat pond,' I say to Tim and Colin when I am in their build area. 'I think where we're going to do the test is like a raging torrent, billions of gallons of water crashing over massive rocks. You really don't want a boat that's a bit tippy, do you?'

'You could be right,' says Colin, which is a very untypical response for an expert. 'I'm very worried about stability. I haven't got enough barrels for the design I had in mind.'

'Oh, I see, that's really annoying…' I say. I have a feeling I know why.

Of course Colin doesn't have enough barrels. The *Scrapheap Challenge* engineering department are on to this sort of thing immediately. Colin will have spoken to assistant producer Jason weeks before flying to LA to take part, and he will have said, 'I need at least twenty barrels to make this thing work.'

The Body Snatchers' 350,000 tonne water skimming speed machine.

'Sure, sure, twenty, OK.'

He may even have added the fatal, 'If I don't have enough barrels, I'll have to redesign on the fly.'

Jason's mind will have ticked over. Giving him exactly what he wants is just too easy; takes the challenge out of the show. He will have called Todd and John and explained the situation; they in turn will have called an American scrap dealer: 'Yo, 'sup?'

'How many of those blue square-shaped steel barrels have you got dude?' Todd will have asked.

"OH NO, HE'S GOING FOR A CATAMARAN."

'About 4,000 already, how many you need, bud?'

'Um, around eight,' says Todd slowly. 'And two of the really heavy mothers.'

'You got it,' says the dealer.

Now, the team look at what they've got. They have managed to dig out every barrel on the site, and it's still not enough for Colin. He stands looking at them, scratching his head.

'We may have to go for a catamaran,' he says eventually.

'Oh no, he's going for a catamaran,' says Jeremy, who is watching from the control tower. 'A catamaran. An unsteerable, top-heavy, ear-splitting metal monster is going to take to the rapids. Excellent.'

'IT'S ALL GOOD FUN'

Jeremy is delighted with the way the teams are working. They are very focused, but when Cathy or I go in to talk with them, they are really funny and ready to help make the programme a good one. The perfect combination.

In the Xtinguishers' build area, what had been a fast start has now become the familiar slow grind. The lads are all suffering from the heat; the temperature, according to Spud's big thermometer that hangs on the back wall of the set, is about 32°C. In the shade. Nice and warm. Steve the judge and I have noticed that when we sit down, the temperature on the throne is in the severe buttock-burn region.

I discuss the Body Snatchers' attitude to the firefighting service with Ian 'Fergie' Fergusson, but he doesn't rise to the bait.

'They call you drip stands, and Trumpton. That's awful, isn't it?'

'It's all good fun.'

'They say you just cut the roof off any car you see at a crash scene, even if there's no one in it.'

'She may have a point,' says Fergie. 'We did cut the roof off the horse box pretty quick.'

'That's true,' I say. As Fergie is talking, I am getting instructions through my earpiece from director Paul to keep winding them up.

'So what do you call paramedics then?'

'We don't have nicknames for them.' He smiles. Clearly he does, but he knows they're unbroadcastable.

When I come out of the build area I am dripping with sweat, and all I've been doing is talking. There is some discussion behind the scenes, and the decision is made to bring in the easy-ups. By now, the easy-ups look like they've been used for artillery practice. They are tattered and twisted to the limit of their use, but we all still struggle into the build area and put them up without losing the tips of any of our fingers. Once the teams can operate in the shade, there is a marked improvement in temperature and, as a result, the work rate, too.

The Xtinguishers' boat is beginning to look just like a boat. The steel roof of the horse box has definitely seen better days, but from watching this team work it's obvious that they will be able to sort out the multiple leak problems.

On the other side, things are looking increasingly big. The engine is already mounted on top of an oil barrel – the huge welded oil barrel catamaran they have lashed together. It looks absurdly high, which apparently it needs to be, as the propeller they have found is enormous.

Another item that has to be planted is any propeller that's needed. I never knew this before I worked on *Scrapheap*, but propellers can be rather dangerous. The tips of a prop blade are moving at very near the speed of sound, hence the enormous amount of noise they can produce. But if they are old, they are generally made of wood, and if they start to disintegrate, bits of propeller can travel a long way at very high speed. Hence, for safety reasons, if a propeller is being used in a challenge, we have to supply a new one. But the crew are wise to the game now, and Body Snatchers' scavengers Debbie and Gerry spend hours searching the yard for the

battered-looking beauty. I say battered-looking. It was such a shiny new propeller blade when it arrived, but John and Todd from the engineering department had a go at 'weathering' it and made it look like a bit of twisted old rubbish. When Gerry arrives proudly sporting the thing, it doesn't look much; but on closer inspection it's worthy of the title 'sculpture'. It really is rather beautiful.

Over lunch, I meet a tall and very charming Canadian man called Tyler

Maybe they're going for the underwater engine approach...

Harcott, who has just been booked to present the American sister show, *Junkyard Wars*. He will be working with the same crew, appearing on screen with Cathy and basically doing exactly the same job as myself. There was a lot of confusion when the previous American presenter appeared on the show. I received loads of e-mails from people asking why I had been sacked. Confusingly, both shows – *Junkyard Wars* and *Scrapheap Challenge* – are shown in the US and on Channel 4 in Britain, but in the US they're both called *Junkyard Wars* and in the UK they're called *Scrapheap Challenge*, unless it's the American one, in which case it's called *Junkyard Wars*. Confused? Join the clan. Basically, if it's Tyler and Cathy, it's the American one; if it's Cathy and I, it's the British one.

Work continues after lunch, frenzied and manic as always. Both teams are quieter, settling in for the long grind of the build. The Body Snatchers' machine just gets bigger and heavier, worrying attributes for a construction that is meant to float. The guards that will protect the world from their madly spinning propeller blade are enormous; the engine itself is a huge great lump, resting eight feet up in the air when the ship, as I now prefer to think of it, is standing on firm ground.

They have found a comfy executive lounger as their pilot's chair, and they work methodically to get all the components fitted. Directly behind the propeller, I watch Debbie construct a pair of 'air rudders', just like the rudder of a boat only bigger, and, obviously, in the air. The idea behind these is that they will steer the boat by pushing the air one way or the other as it's forced past the propeller. I can't help but worry about this, and talk to Steve the judge about it.

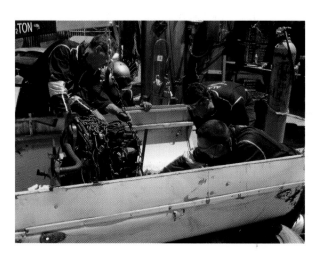

More holes than boat.

'It's utterly hopeless. It'll never even get a chance to work, because the whole thing will sink anyway.'

'And what about the Xtinguishers' upturned horse box roof?'

'Hopeless. They won't be able to steer it when they're going downstream, because you can only steer a jet ski when it's going flat out. But it won't matter, because there are so many holes in the horse box they'll sink before it's a problem.'

We haven't previously had a judge who is so damning of both teams. It makes me want to defend them.

'Oh, they're not that bad. They're both trying really hard.'

'Maybe, but both designs are rubbish. Look at the engine on the Xtinguishers' boat. It's got a drive shaft joining it to the jet ski, but no strengthening around it. If they hit a rock – which they will do – they could bend the shell of the boat, which is only thin and very rusty old steel. Then the drive shaft will get bent and the whole thing could tear itself to bits.'

Fair enough. Say no more.

As we reach the final three hours of the build, we are all grateful to be out of the direct sunlight. Dusk is sudden in Southern California, and soon it starts to get a bit chilly. Not so in the build areas where it's totally manic, noisy, dirty and, if you actually look at what these teams are planning on putting in the water, utterly insane.

I have a chat with the Xtinguishers who are having real problems with their drive system. They have a very reliable Transit van engine, which they are trying to connect to the jet ski thing that will stick out of the back of the horse box. Except they don't have a back on it yet, so it's all theory.

I try to point out the weakness in their design that Steve has described to me, but they can't hear anything now. They have such a huge pile of tasks to complete in such a short time that they're suffering from *Scrap* blindness. As I talk to them, I hear the familiar sound of a V8 starting up, and I rush over to the Body Snatchers' build area. I'm slightly disappointed because they haven't actually mounted their propeller, but they seem very happy with it. At least it works, and as they weld yet more strengthening bars on the vast battleship they are building, it starts to look rather good.

In the final chat with judge Steve, I state that I really like the Body Snatchers' machine. Steve has now changed his tune somewhat, too.

'I think they're both incredible. I can't believe what they've done.'

'So, who's your money on?'

'Oh, I don't want to put any money on either design, but if I really had to, I'd go with the Xtinguishers. At least if they have to abandon ship, they won't be cut up into mincemeat by a massive out-of-control propeller.'

Confidence indeed. I get a signal from Rey Vincenti that time is up, and I announce it to the very grateful teams. They are all exhausted, but sitting proudly in each build area are two of the weirdest-looking waterborne craft we have ever made, and on *Scrapheap Challenge*, that's saying something.

The Test

The day after the manic whitewater racer build, Cathy and I turn up at the yard to record all the links and inserts we haven't been able to do during a normal filming day. The atmosphere is very different, as there's only a skeleton crew attending – one camera operator, one sound technician, and a handful of engineers.

On the day between the build and the test, the machines have to be 'made safe' by the expert from each team and the scrap engineer department. This is made up of Todd and Jesus John, and working around them – constructing start gates, finishing flags and anything else that's decorative and imaginative – is art director Clint. It only took a couple of days before these three blokes were exchanging a constant stream of abuse. They are critical of each other, of everyone else and everything anyone else does, and this seems to make them very happy.

Todd is an enormous lad, over six feet tall, with a slow, lilting delivery. Clint is equally tall, but wiry, and, for a vegetarian hippie, astonishingly verbally aggressive. One night after a long day's shoot, when both Todd and Clint had put in fourteen hours plus on the set, they sat down for an arm wrestle. Of course, what else would you do when you're exhausted and in severe need of a bath? With the powerful size of Todd's arms I would have put money on him to win, but as Cathy pointed out after the bout, Clint has got willpower to spare. They had been goading each other all day.

It was a well-matched dispute. Both are very strong men, but Clint's manic smile and utter determination to win had the edge over Todd's gentle nature in the end. 'Next time dude,' said Todd with a grin.

The engineering department's job after the build day is to make sure that, as far as possible, no one will be injured or killed by their creations when they are put to the test. This usually involves securing the fuel systems, making sure all the welds are sound, making protective shields around fast-moving parts and fitting remote cut-off devices for engines. When you watch a *Scrapheap* machine doing its thing, there is always someone off-camera with a remote control box ready to press the button and kill the engine should something go very wrong. They did so in the monster truck challenge when they realized

Llewellyn has slightly wet feet and demands dry shoes.

Nigel the driver couldn't turn off his massive engine; they were ready to do it when the Catalysts' street sweeper was sucking up tin cans that could have ruptured the tube carrying them to the hopper. They also welded heavy gauge steel sheet all around the Catalysts' vacuum pump housing, because during a test, the clip off a pair of braces had torn a hole in the steel originally used. To give the braces their due, they had survived being flung around at 5,000rpm by the impeller blade. I should check out the brand they clearly won't let you down.

Cathy and I stand around in various locations doing our opening 'pieces to camera' and record a series of inserts for the new *Scrapheap* video. As soon as we've finished we head up Highway 5 towards the Kern river, the location for the following day's shoot.

As we climb out of the valley, we pass various members of the *Scrapheap* crew on the same journey – a huge low-loader truck driven by Jesus John that's taking the machines; a big white van full of costumes and equipment, which is also towing a trailer with the two all-terrain buggies on board; the camera truck; an oversized pick-up pulling a big trailer; and Jason's Jeep, which doesn't have a big load to carry but

The Body Snatchers, ear plugs mandatory.

The Xtinguishers preparing to 'bail in'.

doesn't look like it's going along very happily.

It's dark by the time we get to Bakersfield, which is about halfway to the river. We stop at a garage and ask for directions, because my map-reading is pretty flaky and Cathy doesn't fully trust me to get us there.

An hour later, as we pass a sign that says we're at 6,000 feet, it's clear that she was right to doubt my abilities. We arrive at the location about an hour later than planned, tired, hungry and a little confused. It's very dark as we pull to a halt, but the first people we see are Rey and Andrew, the first and second assistant directors. They have supplied food and beer for everyone and we sit out on their porch listening to the thundering river, which we can't see.

I fall into bed in a little cabin three doors along from them. We have a very early call in the morning and a lot to do.

There has been one other occasion I can remember where I have arrived somewhere late at night having no idea of what the location looks like, only to receive a wonderful shock when I wake up and open the curtains. Last time, it was after a mammoth drive through France. I ended up in the Hotel du Lac, which seemed quite nice at night; but then when I got up and looked out of the window, it was like a scene from *The Sound of Music*. A huge lake – I forget which one, but it was French Alpine, anyway – was right below the window; and in the distance was a range of spectacular snow-capped peaks.

Waking up at the Whispering Pines resort has a very similar effect. I pull back the strip blinds and look out of the window. 'Blimey.'

We are surrounded by mountains, brown and dusty-looking, like something out of a cowboy movie. On the other side of a stand of beautiful trees, crashing through the valley below, is the Kern river. It's big, noisy and everything is astoundingly beautiful. I walk out on to the deck outside my room. We are here for one night and we will be working like mad all day. This is like being given a glimpse of a luxury lifestyle only to be packed off back to the normal world a moment later. It's not fair – I want to stay here longer.

As I meet up with the crew, I'm evidently not the only one. Diana, the production manager, has stayed in the Striesand Suite, actually a beautiful wooden house where Barbara Striesand stayed.

We gather in a trailer park next to the river, which is to be our base for the day. The catering truck is already there and I have a welcome breakfast, dressed in a wetsuit. My first task is to introduce the challenge. This involves me sitting in a rubber boat in the river being held in place by Cathy. In the end, the boat isn't even in the river, it's balanced on a couple of rocks with the river right behind it so it looks like I'm in the river. Fine by me. The water is made up of freshly melted snow, so it isn't exactly balmy.

Cathy and I talk to the teams during their tinker time, which today consists of seeing if the things will actually float. They are far more floaty than I dared expect, and have actually been launched a long way upriver – the only place the truck could access. The safety crew, made up of half-a-dozen Kern River experts who are all from the local area, have guided the machines downriver, buzzing around in little kayaks as if they were born doing it. The machines are floated

Cathy makes sure Robert doesn't get too scared.

Cathy: But it was on fire, wasn't it.
Xtinguishers: Not an actual fire, Cathy, just an intense heat area.

down over the rapids to the area we are using for the race.

After a few final checks, Colin, the Body Snatchers' expert, fires up the 350 cubic inch Chevy engine, which now has the propeller attached – and it's obvious to anyone watching that this thing works. The natural roar of the river is drowned by the brutal man-made roar of a very large engine and a high-speed propeller. The gale the machine is expelling is picking up spray to such an extent that it's soaking people who are watching from the opposite bank. The Body Snatchers are delighted. All that work seems to have paid off.

Next, the Xtinguishers start up their funny looking boat, and again, a torrent of water is fired out of the jet ski. Looks like we've got a race.

Somehow, this small series of events takes up the whole morning. I am always staggered by what happens to time when we are shooting *Scrapheap Challenge*. It just drains away. Everything takes longer than you'd think, and the gaps in between are filled with the constant jabber of the teams and crew. Only director Paul and Jeremy are rushing around worrying that we won't get everything done.

One of the problems the production staff have had with this location was getting permission to use private property. The wonderful man who is helping us cope with the river, Tom Moore, runs a kayak and whitewater rafting company called Sierra South. He owns the strip of river bank we are working from, but not the bank that's right next door, which we also needed to use. We had to go to quite extreme lengths to find places to put cameras and deliver equipment to circumvent the problem. Jason has been up to the location no fewer than four times to try and solve the issue, but he couldn't, and we now have cameras on tripods standing in the rapids. Bit of a nightmare from an insurance perspective, I would imagine.

During the lunchbreak there is much frantic discussion about the final rules of the competition. As always, they have to be made up once we know all the variables. In this case – do the things float? Will they move? Is anyone going to get hurt?

It's decided that it will be a time trial. Neither boat is looking manoeuvrable enough for safe head-to-head racing, so they will each have three runs with different team members at the helm; fastest time wins. This plan is put to the teams, who are all agreeable.

Immediately after lunch, judge Steve and I walk along the sandy path to our position for the race, and I hear more about the Kern river from Tom Moore. He explains that the dusty area we are walking along floods once every fifty years or so, when a truly monster rush of water comes down from the mountains. At its present rate, there's about 3,300 cubic feet of water a second pounding its way through the rounded rocks; at full flow, 140, 000 cubic feet of water a second surge through the valley.

'It's awesome,' says Tom. I imagine it is. I only hope there isn't a sudden increase in water as Steve and I take up our position for the race. It's a pile of rocks at the side of the torrent, backed with a scrap screen built by Clint. Our feet are very wet within moments of getting in place.

Steve and I are on one side of the river; while most of the crew and the teams are on the other, and within minutes the problems of cross-river communication become evident. I am supposed to have an air horn to start the races, but of course it's on the wrong side. However, we've all got walkie-talkies and pretty soon a stout fellow in a little kayak is paddling towards us brandishing the horn.

The Xtinguishers are going to test their boat first, with only expert Alan Pickard at the helm. Both experts are very concerned about safety and don't want to risk the teams, who, to say the least, are extreme novices on whitewater. We watch as the boat starts to move off, and can hear the engine increase revs as he gets it into the full flow of the river.

'It's moving!' says Steve. He is obviously genuinely surprised. 'It's actually moving and not sinking. Blimey!'

It is moving – not fast, but then it is going against the flow of the river. As it nears

'Okay, so when it bursts into flames, you jump out very quickly.'

the turning point, which is close to where we are standing, it rolls about a bit; but Alan makes the turn successfully and floats gently downriver.

'He can steer it too, look at that, great manoeuvrability,' says Steve. He's now really enjoying himself.

'I thought the idea was that it would plane on top of the water,' I say.

'Yes, that was the plan, but it's clearly not going to manage that.'

'Is that smoke?' I ask as Alan steers the boat towards the opposite shore. As we watch in increasing horror, Alan and the boat disappear behind a cloud of dense white smoke. I can't see any flames, but it doesn't look good.

'What's up, Cathy?' I ask over the walkie-talkie.

I have to wait a moment. I can see Cathy standing amongst the teams and the engineering department as they peer through the smoke into the boat.

'It's their flotation foam,' says Cathy eventually. 'They've sprayed loads of it around the exhaust to seal it, and it's more or less caught fire.'

As soon as I hear what they've done, it seems obvious that it's a really bad idea to put inflammable foam all around an exhaust pipe, but I know I would have done the same in the circumstances. Of course, the Xtinguishers are professional firefighters.

Next, the Body Snatchers' machine is pushed into the deeper water, and it floats. It's a little back-heavy, but it seems to be stable. There is no doubting when expert Colin starts the engine, I should think they could hear it in San Francisco, and the area behind the propeller is immediately swamped in white spray.

'This one's moving too, I can't believe it!' says Steve incredulous. 'Would you look at that – amazing.'

Colin powers the enormous machine upriver. The bows are a little low; it doesn't look like this machine is going to plane either, but it's moving. I would make a rough guess that it's actually affecting the downriver water flow, such is the amount of spray coming off the back. I watch as Colin moves the air rudders back and forth, trying to get some form of steering to work. Nothing obvious is happening to the machine, it just seems to be going upriver at an impressive pace; looks like it's a bit faster than the Xtinguishers' up-turned horse box.

As Colin tries to turn around the marker flags, the whole magnificent brutal beauty of the machine starts to fall away. It basically doesn't do steering; it does moving along and making a lot of noise. We hold our breaths as the monster heads right for us. Colin has now given up trying to steer the damn thing, he's killed the engine, has jumped out of the pilot's seat and is digging an oar into the swirling waters to try and get the machine to turn around and head downstream. He almost manages it, but just downstream from where we are standing it thumps into a very big boulder. With a bit of pushing and shoving, he gets it facing the right way, starts it up and covers us in fine spray as it heads downstream. It looks like the currents are having more effect in deciding its course than any theoretical air rudder. It passes the finish line but doesn't stop, it just carries on, engine roaring, until it hits another boulder mid-stream with such force that we can hear it go *thump*.

'I think he's stopped,' says Steve.

I hear over the walkie-talkie from Cathy that the Xtinguishers are going to go for their first timed run while the Body Snatchers are rescuing their machine and dragging it back to the start.

This time, Alan is joined by Xtinguisher team captain Ian West as they take a running start, Steve with stopwatch at the ready. He presses the start button as they pass under the flags that have been strung across the river. As they power their way upstream, the smoke starts to rise again, but this time Ian is leaning over the side of the boat with a bucket.

'Maybe they've got a leak,' says Steve. 'Looks like he's bailing out.'

Looks like they've lost the ignition key again.

The Hairy Rose proves that a horse box roof can really move if you give it enough 'loud pedal'.

We watch closely as they get nearer. I suddenly realize that in fact, Ian is 'bailing in'. He's leaning over the side, filling the bucket and tipping water over the exhaust pipe to stop the foam from bursting into flames.

'They're bailing in! This has to be the first time a crew has bailed water into a boat,' says a delighted Steve. 'I love it, it's totally mad.'

The boat makes the turn point and starts downstream. They have no problem steering this time and they are moving well, even if they are polluting the crisp mountain air with their burning flotation foam.

'Twenty-three seconds,' says Steve. Not bad for a first run up a fast-flowing river in an up-turned horse box roof powered by a battered jet ski and an old Transit van engine.

We have a short wait while half the crew drag the enormous Body Snatchers' machine up the river, but before long I can see that Debbie is at the helm with Colin sitting before her. The engine starts and the spray kicks up. This time they give it a bit more 'loud pedal', as Steve refers to it. The boat – I don't feel comfortable calling it a boat because it doesn't look like one, but anyway – starts to move quite fast. However, the faster it goes, the more the front (counter to expectations and, I'm sure, plans) starts to dig into the water instead of rising above it. This is turning into an air-powered submarine. There is no way this baby is ever going to 'plane' across the surface of the water. Thick custard maybe, but fast-flowing rapids? Not a chance.

They get to the turning point and Debbie starts to wrench at the giant control lever that's attached to the air rudders. Nothing much happens; there's a lot of noise and spray, but no definable turning movement is discernable from the shore. Colin pulls the panic cord and the engine dies. Movement is now entirely due to the flow of water, and the Body Snatchers' giant catamaran starts to float sideways downstream. Debbie and Colin get out their oars and start paddling madly – apparently, to no great effect. They thump into the same boulder as before, just downstream from Steve and I, but manage to get the machine heading in the right direction with a lot of pushing. Debbie starts the engine again and Steve and I are blessed with another fine mist of spray; though we are, it must be said, somewhat protected by Andy, our brave camera operator, who gets soaked.

They pass the finish line in twenty-seven seconds, but of course they don't stop or turn; they head merrily downstream towards some more enormous rocks and slam into them instead.

The final two rounds are carried out in quick succession, a different team member on board with the expert each time. The Xtinguishers achieve pretty much the same time with their second effort, while the Body Snatchers cut five seconds off theirs. They can make it upstream faster than the Xtinguishers, only hampered by their chronic lack of steering capability.

On the Xtinguishers' last run, we see something that by this stage of the game I, for one, had forgotten was even part of the plan. They manage to plane downstream. Fergie is on board, bailing in like a trooper as Alan steers their little horse box roof deftly around the course. Then, as they go for the home run, I hear Alan shout something. Fergie manages to climb over the engine and into the front part of the boat, and yes, sure enough, their speed dramatically increases and the funny looking craft zips across the top of the water at amazing speed. The team on the opposite bank is screaming with delight. They think they've got it. It's a very close-run race, and I turn to Steve to see what time they've made. It's looking pretty good...

Later...

After the celebrations and the ritual champagne soaking, the big clear-up starts. More or less everyone pitches in. I do what I think will be a token amount of equipment-carrying up the steep path from the river to the road, but it ends up being a hard slog for half an hour.

Cathy, Jason and I pile into a car and start

A very loud engine's all you need. And some oars, obviously.

to head downriver. Jason wants to make sure the boats have been successfully lifted out of the water. This makes me reflect that even when I think I'm involved in most aspects of the show's creation, there are always a dozen things going on I have no knowledge of. Of course the boats have to be hauled out of the river, but it never occurred to me.

We pull off the road near the Kernville Bridge which spans the rapids, and find Clint, Jesus John and Todd hauling the machines out of the water with their trusty fork-lift. The low-loader truck is standing by, and a few townspeople have come to see what's going on. They're intrigued by the crudity of the machines that have been charging up and down their river making such a noise all day.

Once Jason has seen the machines safely stowed, we head back to LA. I am heading for Sydney the following day to see my family, and everyone is having a week off before starting the next recording of *Junkyard Wars*. I will be back later in the year to finish the series, but it actually feels like the end now. Many of the crew are leaving and won't be coming back, so there are lots of promises to keep in touch. It's that odd moment when you realize that people you've been working with very intensely will suddenly vanish from your life, possibly for good.

But we have the preliminary rounds of the show in the can. Now it's just a matter of editing the material into a programme we can all watch. This, however, is just as much of a monster task, but involving fewer people. Back in London, the director and editor will review something like eighty hours of tape for each programme, which will have to be cut down to fifty minutes.

That's all, for now...
How about a whitewater monster torpedo river cleaner?

The first time I'll see it will be when I do the commentary, stuck in a little booth with headphones on. Four series on, and I have completely forgotten how I got tangled up with such a charming bunch of nutters. I wouldn't have missed it for the world.

TIME TEAM
COLLECTION

This latest **Time Team** book will be illustrated throughout with specially commissioned photographs of six new sites, and is a fascinating portrait of life on location as part of the **Time Team**. Tieing in to the ninth series of **Time Team**. Available from 9 November priced £18.99.

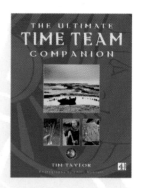

Tim Taylor draws on the expertise of the **Time Team** contributors to answer all your questions about the programme, including a guide to fifty excavation sites illustrating our history from the dawn of time to the modern age. Available now priced £12.99.

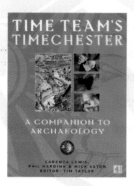

Time Team's Timechester: A Family Guide to Archaeology is an imaginatively created book which has a dual purpose: it is a history of British settlement and an intrduction to archaeological methods. Available now priced £16.99.

Behind the Scenes at Time Team looks at the work that goes in to making the series: how the sites are chosen, what life is like during the three-day digs and the most exciting finds. Available now priced £12.99.

All available directly from the Channel 4 Shop.
Please phone 0870 744 44 44 or write to The Channel 4 Shop, 33 Park Royal Road, London, NW10 7LN